书虫·牛津英汉对照读物

织工马南

Silas Marner

George Eliot

Clare West　改写
邹晓明　译

外语教学与研究出版社
牛津大学出版社

(京)新登字 155 号

京权图字 01-97-0350

图书在版编目(CIP)数据

织工马南：英汉对照/(英)艾略特(Eliot, G.)著；(英)韦斯特(West, C.)改写；邹晓明译. - 北京：外语教学与研究出版社，1997
(书虫·牛津英汉对照读物)
ISBN 7-5600-1358-9

Ⅰ.织… Ⅱ.①艾… ②韦… ③邹… Ⅲ.小说-英国-对照读物-英、汉 Ⅳ.H319.4：Ⅰ

中国版本图书馆 CIP 数据核字(97)第 24291 号

织工马南

著 George Eliot
改写 Clare West
译 邹晓明
* * *
外语教学与研究出版社出版发行
(北京西三环北路 19 号)
中国人民解放军第 1201 工厂印刷
新华书店总店北京发行所经销
开本 850×1092 1/32 4.375 印张
1998 年 10 月第 1 版 1998 年 10 月第 1 次印刷
印数：1—31000 册
* * *
ISBN 7-5600-1358-9/H·765
定价：4.90 元

简 介

在19世纪早期的英国僻静的乡村，生活有着一成不变的模式。四季交替，对于住在大房子里的乡绅及其全家和对于住在小草屋里的村民们来说都是一样的。任何新鲜和古怪的事情在像瑞福洛这样的村庄里都会遭到猜疑。

织工西拉斯·马南就很古怪。他独自居住，没人知道他的家庭情况。如果你不知道他的父母是谁你怎么能够信任他呢？他脸色苍白，眼神怪异，并且总是瞪着眼睛，因为他每天都要在织机上干很长时间的活，甚至星期天也干，而星期天他应该去教堂。他一定是魔鬼的朋友，村民们相互这么说。

可怜的西拉斯！他是一个忧伤、孤独的人，他唯一的朋友就是那些闪光的金币，那是他织布挣来的，被他藏在地板下面。但是变故总会发生，即使在瑞福洛这样安静的村庄里。乡绅的两个儿子之间有一个秘密，这导致争吵、抢夺，以及死亡。那是在一个下雪的夜晚，在离西拉斯的草屋不远的地方……

乔治·艾略特(1819—1880)是英国最伟大的小说家之一，她真名叫玛丽·安·埃文斯。她生前就以小说创作而著名，主要作品包括《织工马南》、《米德尔马奇》和《弗罗斯河上的磨坊》。

1

Silas Marner, past and present

In the early years of the nineteenth century, strange-looking little men were often seen on the country roads, usually with a heavy bag on their shoulders. They were linen-weavers, taking the linen they had woven to the women in the villages. Unlike the strong, healthy country people, they were small and thin, with tired white faces, bent backs and round shoulders. They were often shortsighted too, because they had to look so closely at their work. To the villagers the weavers looked almost foreign, and quite frightening. Where did they come from? Was it the devil who sent them? Who were their parents? How could you trust a man if you didn't know his father or mother? Country people used to be very suspicious of all strangers and travellers. They were also suspicious of clever people, people who could do something they themselves had not learnt to do. That is why the linen-weavers, who often moved from towns to live and work in the country, were considered strangers all their lives by their neighbours, and were sometimes very lonely as a result.

Silas Marner was one of these weavers. He lived in a small cottage near the village of Raveloe. Every day he worked at his loom in the cottage. The small boys of Raveloe had never heard the sound of a loom before, and sometimes they used to run up to his house to look quickly in at the window. If Silas noticed

1 马南的过去和现在

在19世纪初的英国，人们经常在乡村小路上看到一些小个子男人，扛着沉沉的大袋子，样子很古怪。他们是织布匠，在把织好的亚麻布送给乡下妇女。和健壮的乡下人不同，织工们身材瘦小而且脸色苍白，神情疲惫，曲背弯腰。由于用眼过度，他们中许多人眼睛都有些近视。在乡下人眼里，这些织布匠几乎算得上怪异，而且很吓人。乡下人疑惑不解：这些人是从哪里来的？是魔鬼派他们来的吗？他们的父母是谁呢？一个你不了解他父母的人，你怎么能信任呢？乡下人常常怀疑所有的陌生人和旅客。他们也怀疑那些聪明的人，那些会干一些乡下人自己不会做的事的人。因为这个原因，这些从城市搬到乡下干活、居住的织工终生都会被邻居认为是怪人，并因而感到很孤独。

西拉斯就是这些织工中的一个。他住在靠近瑞福洛村的一间小草屋里，每天在小屋里的织布机上干活。瑞福洛村的孩子们以前从没有听到过织布机的声音，所以经常到他的小屋来扒窗户偷看。如果西拉斯发

linen *n. a special kind of cloth (more like cotton than wool)* 亚麻布。**weaver** *n. a person who make cloth* 织工。**bent** *a.* 弯曲的。**suspicious** *a. not believing or trusting someone* 猜疑的，疑心的。**loom** *n. a machine for weaving cloth* 织机。

them, he lifted his shortsighted eyes from the loom to stare at the boys. There was something terrible about his stare, which made the boys run away at once, screaming with fear. The villagers believed that Silas had an almost devilish power, which he could use to harm them if he wanted, and so they were all afraid of him. Raveloe was an important-looking village with a fine old church and a number of large farms. But it was at least an hour away from any other village, and very few strangers visited it, which explains why the villagers' opinions were so out of date.

Silas Marner had first come to Raveloe fifteen years before, as a young man. He and his way of life seemed very strange to the villagers. He worked long hours at his loom, and had no friends or visitors from the village or anywhere else. He never talked to his neighbours unless it was necessary for his work, and he never looked at any of the Raveloe girls. 'Who would want to marry him anyway?' the girls laughed to each other. 'Marry a dead man come to life again, with that unhealthy white skin and those insect-like eyes of his? Certainly not!'

One of the villagers had had a strange experience with Silas. One evening he had discovered the weaver resting on a field gate, his eyes open but unseeing, and his body cold and hard, like a dead man's. After a few moments Silas appeared to wake up, said 'Good night', and walked away.

When this was discussed in the village, some people thought that Silas had had a fit. But others, like Mr Macey, the church

觉了,就会把近视眼从织布机上抬起来盯着孩子们。他的眼光中似乎有什么可怕的东西,孩子们马上惊叫着四散跑开。村里人有些怕他,因为大家相信西拉斯有着近乎魔鬼的力量,如果愿意他可以用来伤害他们。瑞福洛是一个很气派的村庄,有着很好的老式教堂和大片的农田。但由于离最近的邻村也有一个小时的路程,很少有陌生人来,所以村里人的思想非常落后。

西拉斯·马南是15年前到瑞福洛来的,那时他还是一个小伙子。他和他的生活方式对瑞福洛的村民来说是那么神秘。他长时间在织布机上工作,没有朋友和客人。除非为了工作的事,他从不和邻居说话,也从不看一眼瑞福洛村的女孩子们。“有谁愿意嫁给他?”姑娘们互相开玩笑,“有谁愿意嫁给这个苍白得吓人,长着一双虫子一样眼睛的人?好像死人刚活过来一样!谁也不会愿意!”

一个村民目睹过一件怪事。一天晚上,他发现西拉斯在一个门口歇着,眼睛睁着但目光呆滞,身体又凉又硬,就像一个死人。过了一会儿,西拉斯看上去醒了过来,说了一句“晚安”,然后就离开了。

当村里人议论这件事的时候,有的人认为西拉斯是病了,但有的人,像教堂的执事

scream *v. give a loud, sharp cry* 尖叫。**develish** *a. like a devil* 魔鬼般的。**insect** *n.* 昆虫。**discuss** *v. have conversation about, talk about* 讨论。**fit** *n. a sudden illness, when a person is unconscious for a time* (病的)发作。

clerk, refused to accept a medical explanation.

'No, he isn't ill, that weaver,' said old Mr Macey, shaking his head knowingly. 'If he had a fit, he'd fall down, wouldn't he? I think his soul flies out of his body sometimes and that's why he looks so strange. He doesn't come to church, does he? And how does he know so much about medicines? You all remember how he made Sally Oates better, when the doctor himself could do no more for her. That's the devil's work, believe me!'

However, the housewives needed Silas to weave their linen, and they could find nothing wrong with his work. The years passed, and Raveloe villagers did not change their opinion of the weaver. At the end of fifteen years they said exactly the same things about him, but they believed them more strongly. They also said that he had saved up a lot of money since he had come to Raveloe.

Silas had come from a large town to the north of Raveloe. Here he had lived a very different life. Because he was one of a large number of weavers, he was not considered strange, and he belonged to an enthusiastic religious group. They met every Sunday at the chapel in Light Street. Once, at a chapel meeting, Silas had become unconscious and had sat without moving, hearing or seeing, for over an hour. This experience made him specially interesting to the rest of the group.

'We should not call this strange unconsciousness a fit,' the minister, Mr Paston, told them. 'No, it's much more than

麦西先生，拒绝接受这种医学的解释。

“不，那个织布匠不是病了，”麦西老先生有把握地摇着头说，“如果病了，他会倒下，对吧？我觉得他的灵魂有时会离开他的身体，所以他才会看起来那么奇怪。他不上教堂，对吧？而且他怎么会知道那么多医疗的事？你们都记得吧，医生都没办法，他却能让萨莉·奥茨好过一点。相信我，他那是妖术！”

然而不管怎样，主妇们需要西拉斯为她们织亚麻布，他的货无可挑剔。时间一年年过去，可人们对西拉斯的看法从来没有改变。15年后，人们仍在议论着同样的事，只不过更相信这些事了。同时他们还说西拉斯来瑞福洛以后已积攒了一笔可观的财富。

西拉斯是从瑞福洛北面的一个大镇子来的，在那里他过着与现在完全不同的生活。作为众多织工中的一个，他很平常，而且他属于一个活跃的宗教组织。教友们每个礼拜日都在日光街的小教堂集会。在一次集会中，西拉斯突然失去了知觉，坐在那里一动不动，听不到也看不到，长达一个多小时。这次经历使教友们觉得他很特别。

“我们不应该认为他这种奇怪的失去知觉是疾病，”牧师帕斯通先生告诉大家，“完

housewife *n*. *woman directing household affairs* 家庭妇女。**enthusiastic** *a*. *having strong interest* 积极的。**unconscious** *a*. 没有知觉的。**minister** *n*. （基督教的）牧师。**chapel** *n*. *a room or building used for religious meetings* 小教堂。

that. In that moment, when he is absent from us, our young friend Silas's soul is *open*, open to a possible message from God. I believe he has been chosen by God!'

Silas's best friend at chapel was William Dane, a serious young man who was, some people thought, a little too sure of his own goodness and cleverness. Silas, however, could see no fault in him, and trusted his friend completely. They remained good friends, when Silas became engaged to a young woman, Sarah, who belonged to the same chapel. In fact Silas was delighted that Sarah did not mind if William joined them sometimes on their Sunday walks.

Strangely, when Silas had his fit at the chapel meeting, William was the only one who disagreed with the minister.

'To me it looks more like the devil's work than God's,' William had said. 'Look deep into yourself, friend Silas. Is there any evil hiding in your soul?'

Silas was hurt that his friend doubted him, and he began to be worried, too, about Sarah. She seemed to be showing signs of dislike towards him, but when he asked her about it, she did not give him any answer.

At that time one of the chapel leaders was dangerously ill, and because he had no family, some of the young men offered to sit with him at night. One night Silas was sitting alone at the old man's bedside. Time seemed to pass slowly in the quiet, dark room. But suddenly he realized that the man was no longer breathing. He was dead.

全不是这样。他的意识离开我们的时候，我们年轻的朋友西拉斯的灵魂打开了，去接受上帝的信息。我相信是上帝选择了他。”

西拉斯在教会最要好的朋友是威廉·戴恩，一个严肃的年轻人，有的人认为他对自己的聪明善良未免太有把握。但是西拉斯却不认为他的朋友有任何缺点，他完全信任威廉。当西拉斯与同教会的年轻女子萨拉订婚以后，威廉还是他最要好的朋友。西拉斯很高兴萨拉不介意俩人的礼拜日散步有时有威廉在场。

奇怪的是，在西拉斯发病以后，威廉却是唯一一个不同意牧师观点的人。

“依我看不像是上帝倒像是魔鬼干的，”威廉说，“好好看看你自己，西拉斯，我的朋友，是不是有魔鬼隐藏在你的灵魂里？”

被好朋友怀疑使西拉斯很伤心，同时，他也开始为萨拉担起心来。萨拉似乎开始显得有点不太喜欢他了。可当西拉斯问起来，她却又什么也不说。

这个时候，一位教会的长老生了重病。因为他没有家室，教会的年轻人就轮流在晚上陪伴他。一天晚上，西拉斯独自一人陪坐在老人的床边。在黑暗而安静的屋子里，时间似乎过得很慢。突然，西拉斯意识到老人已经停止了呼吸，已经死了。

absent *a*. *being away* 离开的。**delighted** *a*. *happy*, *pleased* 高兴的。**sign** *n*. 征兆，迹象。

'Strange!' thought Silas. 'His body's cold! He's been dead for some time! Why didn't I notice? Perhaps I've had another fit. And it's already four o'clock in the morning. Why hasn't William come? He promised he'd come at two o'clock!' He hurried out of the house to call the doctor and the minister, and then went to work as usual, still wondering why William had not arrived.

But that evening, after work, William came to his room, with the minister. They were both looking very serious.

'You must come to the chapel at once,' said Mr Paston.

'But why?' asked Silas, looking unhappily at them.

'You will hear when you get there,' was the only answer.

Then, in the chapel, Silas stood alone, in front of all the people who were once his friends. The room was silent. There was a pocket-knife in the minister's hand.

'Where did you leave this knife?' he asked.

Silas was trembling at this strange question. 'I don't remember,' he answered.

'Silas, Silas, you must confess!' cried the minister. 'Tell us the truth! This knife, *your* knife, was found at the dead man's bedside, and the bag of church money, which I saw there myself only yesterday, has gone!'

Silas did not speak for a moment. Then he said, 'God knows I did not steal the money. Search my room—you won't find the money. I'm not a thief.'

'You were the only one in our dead friend's house last

"奇怪!"西拉斯想,"他的身体已经凉了。他已经死了一会儿了! 我怎么没有注意? 我可能又犯病了。已经是早上4点了,威廉为什么还没有来换班? 他说会在2点钟到的!"他跑出屋去喊大夫和牧师,然后像平时一样去工作,他一直不明白为什么威廉没有按时来换班。

这天晚上下班以后,威廉和牧师一起来到了西拉斯的屋子。两个人都很严肃。

"你必须马上到教堂去。"帕斯通先生说。

"为什么?"西拉斯不太高兴地看着他们。

"到那儿你就知道了。"这是唯一的回答。

然后,在教堂里,西拉斯独自一人站在他以前的朋友们面前。屋里很静。牧师的手里拿着一把小刀。

"你把这把刀放在哪儿了?"他问。

西拉斯被这个奇怪的问题吓了一跳。"我不记得了。"

"西拉斯,西拉斯,你必须坦白!"牧师叫道,"向我们坦白事实! 你的这把刀是在死者的床旁发现的,而且教会的钱袋也不见了,我昨天还看见它在那里!"

西拉斯半晌说不出话来。终于他说:"上帝知道我没有偷钱。去搜查我的房间吧——你们不会找到钱。我不是贼。"

"威廉告诉我们他突然病了,不能去接

promise *v*. 许诺,发誓。**pocket-knife** *n*. 随身携带的小折刀。**confess** *v*. *to tell the truth about something wrong that you have done* 供认,坦白。

night, when the money was stolen,' said Mr Paston. 'William tells us he was suddenly ill, which prevented him from coming to take your place. We will search your room.'

And when they went to Silas's room, William found the missing bag, now empty, under Silas's bed.

'Silas, my friend,' cried William, 'confess your crime to us now! Send the devil away from your soul!'

Silas turned to the man he had always trusted. 'William, in the nine years since we've been friends, have I ever told you a lie? But God will prove the truth.'

As he looked at William, he suddenly remembered something, and reddened. He said in a trembling voice, 'The knife wasn't in my pocket last night!'

'I don't know what you mean,' replied William coldly.

In the strange little world of the Light Street chapel, they did not believe in the law or judges. They thought only God knew the answers, so they agreed to draw lots to decide what had happened. They all went down on their knees to ask for God's help in finding the truth. Silas knelt with them, sure that God would prove his honesty. There was silence, as the minister took one of the papers out of the covered box.

'*The lots say that Silas Marner has stolen the money*,' he said. 'You will leave the chapel, Silas Marner, and you will not be accepted back until you confess your crime.'

Silas listened in horror. At last he walked over to William Dane and said firmly, 'I lent you my knife, you know that.

你的班,所以你是昨天晚上唯一在我们死去的朋友房间的人,就是那时钱被偷了,"帕斯通先生说。"我们要搜查你的房间。"

到了西拉斯的房间,威廉在西拉斯的床底下发现了丢失的、已经空了的钱袋。

"西拉斯,我的朋友,"威廉喊道,"快向我们认罪吧!把你灵魂中的魔鬼赶走吧!"

西拉斯转向这个他曾经信赖的朋友。"威廉,在我们做朋友的9年里我有没有对你说过谎?上帝会证明事实。"

看着威廉,西拉斯突然想起来了什么,脸红起来。"刀子昨晚不在我的兜里!"西拉斯颤抖地说。

"我不明白你的意思,"威廉冷冷地回答。

在日光街小教堂这个奇特的小世界里,人们不相信法律和法官。他们认为只有上帝知道事情的答案,所以他们一致同意通过抽签来判断到底发生了什么。于是大家都跪下祈求上帝帮助查出事实真相。西拉斯和大家一同跪着,他相信上帝会证明他是诚实的。牧师从盖着的盒子里抽出一张纸的时候,屋子里一片寂静。

"签上说是西拉斯·马南偷了钱,"他说,"西拉斯·马南,你得离开教堂。在你认罪前,我们不会再接纳你。"

西拉斯恐怖地听着。最后他走到威廉·戴恩的面前坚定地说:"我把刀子借给你了,你

prevent *v. stop or hinder* 防止,阻止。**tremble** *v. shake involuntarily* 发抖,颤抖。**draw lots** 抽签。

You stole the money, while I was having a fit, and you've blamed me for it. But perhaps you'll never be punished, since there is no God who takes care of the good and punishes the bad, only a God of lies.'

'You hear, my friends?' said William, smiling sadly. 'This is the voice of the devil speaking.'

Silas went home. The next day he sat alone for the whole day, too miserable to do anything. On the second day the minister came to tell him that Sarah had decided she could not marry him. Only a month later, Sarah married William Dane, and soon afterwards Silas Marner left the town.

At Raveloe, Silas shut himself away in his cottage. He did not want to think about the disaster he had experienced. He could not understand why God had refused to help him. But now that his trust in God and his friends had been broken, he did not feel strong enough to build up that trust again, in a new church and with new friends. From now on, he would live in a dark, loveless, hopeless world.

All that was left to him was his weaving, and he sat at his loom seven days a week, working all the daylight hours. In the town he had earned less, and had given much of his money to the chapel, for the old, the poor, and the sick. But now he began to earn more than ever before, and there was no reason for him to give away any of it. He was often paid for his linen in gold. He discovered that he liked holding the shining coins in his hand and looking at their bright faces.

知道的。你趁我发病的时候偷了钱，并以此陷害我。不过你可能永远也不会受到惩罚，因为根本没有一个保护善良惩治邪恶的上帝，只有一个说谎的上帝。"

"朋友们，听到了吧？"威廉苦笑着说，"这就是魔鬼的声音。"

西拉斯回到家里，第二天他在屋里呆了一整天，痛苦得不能做任何事。第三天牧师来告诉他萨拉决定取消与他的婚约。一个月后，萨拉嫁给了威廉·戴恩。再后来不久，西拉斯离开了这个镇子。

在瑞福洛，西拉斯把自己关在小草屋里。他不愿意再去想那些痛苦的经历。他不明白为什么上帝拒绝帮助他。现在他的对上帝和朋友的信任都已经崩溃了，他已经没有足够的信心再到新的教堂去和新的朋友一起重建这种信任。从此，他要开始生活在一个黑暗的、没有爱也没有希望的世界里。

西拉斯剩下的只有织布。他一个礼拜7天都坐在织布机前面从早到晚地工作。在城里时他挣的不多，而且大部分捐给了教会，去帮助老人、穷人和病人。但现在他挣的比以前多许多，而且也没有理由再给出去。顾客经常付给他金币，他发现自己喜欢把闪光的金币拿在手里，看它们闪亮的表面。

blame *v. find fault with* 责备。**punish** *v.* 惩罚。**miserable** *a. very unhappy* 痛苦的。**shut oneself away** *close the door and stay alone* 关起来。**disaster** *n. great or sudden misfortune* 灾难。

In his childhood, Silas had been taught, by his mother, to make simple medicines from wild flowers and plants. One day he saw the shoemaker's wife, Sally Oates, sitting at her cottage door, and he realized she had all the signs of the illness which had killed his mother. He felt sorry for Sally, and although he knew he could not prevent her dying, he prepared some medicine for her which made her feel much better. The villagers considered this a good example of Silas's strange, frightening power, but as it had worked for Sally, they started visiting Silas to ask for help with their own illnesses. But Silas was too honest to take their money and give them useless medicine. He knew he had no special power, and so he sent them away. The villagers believed he was refusing to help them, and they were angry with him. They blamed him for accidents that happened to them, and deaths in the village. So poor Silas's kindness to Sally did not help him make friends in Raveloe.

But little by little, the piles of gold coins in his cottage grew higher. The harder he worked, the less he spent on himself. He counted the coins into piles of ten, and wanted to see them grow into a square, and then into a larger square. He was delighted with every new coin, but it made him want another. His gold became a habit, a delight, a reason for living, almost a religion. He began to think the coins were his friends, who made the cottage less lonely for him. But it was only at night, when he had finished his work, that he spent time with them. He kept them in two bags, under the floorboards near the loom.

小的时候，西拉斯的妈妈教过他用野花、野草制作一些简单的药材。一天，西拉斯看见鞋匠的老婆萨莉·奥茨坐在家门口，看得出她已经染上了夺去他母亲生命的那种病。西拉斯很为萨莉难受，虽然知道自己没有能力救活她，西拉斯还是为她配了些药使她减少一些痛苦。村民们认为这是一个很好的例子，可以说明西拉斯的神奇而可怕的力量，但是因为这种力量在萨莉身上产生了效果，人们开始纷纷找上门来请西拉斯给自己诊病。然而西拉斯太诚实了，不愿意收了钱而把没用的药卖给别人。他知道自己没有超人的力量，于是就把人们都轰了出去。村民们认为是西拉斯不愿意帮助大家，都很生气，于是把自己遇到的灾难和村里发生的死亡都归罪于他。因此对萨莉的善行没有帮助西拉斯在瑞福洛交到朋友。

慢慢地，西拉斯的金币越码越高。他干活越卖力，为自己花钱就越少。他把金币每10个码成一摞，想像着它们变成一片，再变成一大片。每一枚新的金币都使他高兴，也使他更渴望得到下一枚金币。他的金币成了一种爱好，一种喜悦，一个活着的原因，甚至成了一种宗教。他开始认为金币是他的朋友，它们使他在小屋里不再那么寂寞。但只有在晚上，结束了一整天的工作，他才有时间陪伴它们。他把它们放在织布机旁边

refuse *v. say 'no' to a request or offer* 拒绝。**square** *n. plane figure with four equal sides and four right angles* 方形。**floorboard** *n.*一块地板（常指可掀起的活动地板）。

Like a thirsty man who needs a drink, he took them out every evening to look at them, feel them, and count them. The coins shone in the firelight, and Silas loved every one of them. When he looked at his loom, he thought fondly of the half-earned gold in the work he was doing, and he looked forward to the years ahead of him, the countless days of weaving and the growing piles of gold.

地板下的两只袋子里。像干渴的人需要喝水一样,他每天晚上都要把它们拿出来看一看,摸一摸,数一数。金币在炉火的照耀下闪闪发光,西拉斯爱它们当中的每一个。每当看到织布机,西拉斯都满怀爱怜地想到即将在工作中挣到的金币,并且想到今后数不清的工作的日子和将会越堆越高的金币。

fondly *ad*. 喜爱地,爱怜地。**half-earned** *a*. 快要挣到的。**countless** *a*. 数不尽的,无数的。

2
Godfrey and Dunstan Cass

The most important person in Raveloe was Squire Cass, a gentleman farmer, who lived with his three sons in the handsome Red House opposite the church, and owned a number of farms outside the village. His wife had died many years before.

One dark November evening, fifteen years after Silas Marner had first arrived in Raveloe, some of the villagers were drinking beer in the public house, the Rainbow. Old Mr Macey, the church clerk, was remembering the Squire's wife.

'She was a wonderful lady,' he said, shaking his grey head sadly. 'Everything was always so pretty and clean at the Red House when she was alive! When she died, all those years ago, the poor Squire, well, he didn't know *what* to do. And he's still lonely, believe me! That's why we often see him in here in the evenings. And another thing, if poor Mrs Cass were alive today, I'm sure she'd be very disappointed with her sons. The Squire should make those boys do some work, but instead he lets them stay at home and gives them money to spend on horses, or gambling, or women!'

'Come, come, Mr Macey,' said the landlord. 'They're rich young gentlemen, after all. You can't expect them to work on the farms like us country people. But you're right about Dunstan Cass. He's a bad one, he is. Always borrowing money, and

2 戈弗雷·凯斯和邓斯坦·凯斯

瑞福洛村最重要的人物是乡绅凯斯。他的妻子许多年前就已经死了，只有他和3个儿子一起住在教堂对面的漂亮的"红屋"里，在村子外面有大片属于他的土地。

11月的一个傍晚，在西拉斯·马南来到瑞福洛村15年以后，几个村民在名叫"彩虹"的小酒馆里喝酒，教堂的执事麦西老先生讲起了凯斯的妻子。

"那是个好女人，"麦西伤感地摇着长满灰发的头，"她在的时候，红屋从来都是那么干净、漂亮！许多年前，她去世的时候，可怜的乡绅，唉，他不知道该怎么办。现在，他仍然很孤独，真的！所以我们才会经常见他晚上到这儿来喝酒。如果凯斯太太还活着，她一定会为她的儿子们感到失望。乡绅应该让他的儿子们去干点儿活，而不应该让他们呆在家里，还给他们钱去玩马、赌博、找女人！"

"行了，麦西先生，"酒馆主人说，"不管怎么说，人家是有钱的年轻绅士，你哪能让他们像我们这些乡下人一样下地干活呢？不过邓斯坦·凯斯倒确实像你说的，他确实不怎么样，总在借钱，却从来不还，总是赌博，

squire *n. the title for the most important gentleman or landowner in a country area (not used now)* 乡绅，大地主。**opposite** *a. facing* 在……对面。**rainbow** *n.* 彩虹。

never paying it back. Always gambling, always in trouble! He'll come to a bad end, he will!'

'But the other two are different,' said the butcher, a red-faced, smiling man. 'Bob Cass is still only a boy. And Mr Godfrey, the eldest, well, I don't believe he'll be like his brother Dunstan. Just look at him! He's got an open, honest face. And he's going to inherit the Squire's money and all the land. And what's more, he's going to marry Miss Nancy Lammeter. When she moves into the Red House as Mrs Godfrey Cass, she'll make life more comfortable for all the Casses. She'll save the Squire money too—the Lammeters have the best of everything in their house, but they're very careful with their money.'

The farrier, a small man with a sharp face, always enjoyed disagreeing with the butcher. 'Mr Godfrey marry Miss Nancy!' he laughed. 'That's what *you* think! Haven't you noticed how Miss Nancy has changed towards Godfrey since last year? You remember, he was away from home, for days and days. Nobody knows what he was doing, but Godfrey hasn't been the same since then. Miss Nancy isn't stupid—she won't marry a man she can't trust!'

The landlord always tried to prevent his customers from arguing. 'What you all say is very true. But let's hope that Mr Godfrey doesn't lose his chance of marrying Miss Nancy.'

Meanwhile, at the Red House, Godfrey Cass was waiting for his brother in the sitting-room, with a very worried expression

而且总是惹麻烦！他一定不会有好下场！”

“另两个可不一样，”笑眯眯的红脸屠户说，“鲍勃·凯斯还是个孩子，老大戈弗雷先生可不像他兄弟邓斯坦，看看他那张脸是多么的诚实、大方。他会继承乡绅的财产和所有的土地，而且他还会娶南茜·拉默特小姐。等她以戈弗雷·凯斯太太的身份入主红屋后，她会把凯斯全家的生活照料好。而且她会为乡绅节省很多钱——拉默特家有各种最好的东西，可他们用钱很小心。”

长着尖脸的小个子马掌匠最爱和屠户过不去。“戈弗雷先生娶南茜小姐！”他大笑着说，“这是你这么想！你没发现从去年开始南茜小姐对戈弗雷的态度已经变了吗？你知道，他经常离开家外出，一去好多天。没人知道他在干什么，可从那时起他就变了。南茜小姐可不傻——她不会嫁给一个她把握不住的人。”

酒馆主人总是试图平息客人们的争论。“你们说的都对，但愿戈弗雷先生不要失去娶南茜小姐的机会。”

在大家在酒馆谈论的同时，在红屋里，戈弗雷·凯斯正在客厅中等他的弟弟邓斯坦，他英俊的脸上一脸焦急。一会儿，门开

comfortable *a. giving comfort to the body* 舒适的。**farrier** *n. someone who puts new shoes on horses* 钉马蹄铁的铁匠。

on his handsome face. Soon the door opened, and a heavy-looking young man entered. It was Dunstan. He had clearly been drinking.

'How I hate him!' thought Godfrey.

'Well, *sir*,' said Dunstan unpleasantly, 'you sent for me, and as you're the oldest, and you'll be the Squire one day, I have to obey you. So what do you want?'

'Just listen, will you?' replied Godfrey angrily, 'if you aren't too drunk to understand! You must pay me back the money I lent you last month. You know I got it from Fowler, of Church Farm. He owed the money to the Squire, and asked me to give it to him. Now the Squire is angry with Fowler for not paying, and I've *got* to give the money back!'

Dunstan came close to Godfrey and smiled in an evil way. 'Well, my dear kind brother, why don't you find the money *yourself*? That would be much less trouble for me!'

Godfrey controlled himself with difficulty. 'Don't smile at me like that, or I'll hit you!'

'Oh no, you won't,' answered Dunstan. 'Because if you do, I'll tell the Squire your secret. I'll tell him that his handsome eldest son fell in love with that poor girl Molly in the town, and married her in a hurry. The Squire'll be angry because you married her in secret, and he'll disinherit you. Then *I'll* get the house and land when the old man dies! But don't worry, I'm a good brother to you. I won't tell him, and you'll find the money to pay back, I know you will.'

了，一个粗壮的年轻人走进来。这就是邓斯坦，他显然刚喝过许多酒。

“我太恨他了！”戈弗雷心里想。

“啊，先生，”邓斯坦不高兴地说，“你派人叫我，因为你是老大，因为有一天你会成为乡绅，所以我不能不听命于你。你想干什么？”

“如果还没醉得听不懂话你就好好听着！”戈弗雷生气地说，“你必须把我上个月借给你的钱还给我。你知道我是从教堂农场的福勒那里拿的钱，他这些钱是欠咱们父亲的，他让我把这钱还给父亲。现在父亲以为福勒还没有还钱，所以很生气，我必须把钱还回去！”

邓斯坦走近戈弗雷阴险地笑了。“好吧，我亲爱的好心的哥哥，你为什么不自己去找钱？那就不会太麻烦我了！”

戈弗雷努力控制住自己。“别这么对我笑，否则我揍你！”

“不，你不会，”邓斯坦回答，“因为如果你揍了我，我就会向父亲告发你的秘密。我会告诉他，他的漂亮的长子爱上了城里的一个穷丫头莫丽，而且匆匆忙忙娶了她。父亲会因为你偷偷娶了她而生气的，并且会取消你的继承权。那么我将在老头儿死后得到这房子和土地！不过别担心，我是你的好兄弟，我不会告诉他，而且你会自己找到钱还回去，我知道你会的。”

obey *v. do one is told to do* 听从。**owe** *v. be in debt to (sb.) or for (sth.)* 欠（钱等）。**control** *v. have the power to order or direct* 控制。**disinherit** *v. take away the right to inherit* 剥夺……的继承权。

'Where can I get the money from?' cried Godfrey. 'I tell you, I haven't got any!'

'You could borrow it,' said Dunstan carelessly. 'Or wait—I've had a better idea. You could sell your horse.'

'Sell Wildfire! You know how much I love that horse!'

'Well, you could ride him to the hunt tomorrow. I know two or three men who'd be interested in buying him, and they'll be at the hunt, I'm sure. It'd be easy.'

'No, I haven't got time to go hunting tomorrow. I—I'm going to Mrs Osgood's birthday dance.'

'Aha!' said Dunstan, laughing. 'And perhaps you'll see sweet Miss Nancy there—and you'll dance with her—and you'll talk of love...'

'Be quiet!' shouted Godfrey, his face turning red. 'Don't speak of Miss Nancy like that, or I'll kill you!'

'Don't get so angry, brother,' answered Dunstan calmly. 'You've got a very good chance with her. In fact, I advise you to be nice to her. You and I know that Molly's started drinking. Well, if she drinks too much one day and dies, then you could marry Nancy. She wouldn't mind being a second wife, if she didn't know there was a first. And luckily you've got a kind brother who'll keep your secret well.'

Godfrey's face was white now, and he was trembling. 'Look, Dunstan, I've nearly had enough of this. You can push a man too far, you know. Perhaps I'll go to the Squire now and confess everything to him. He'll discover the truth one day,

"我到哪儿去弄钱?"戈弗雷喊道,"告诉你,我没钱!"

"你可以去借,"邓斯坦漫不经心地说,"或者,等等——我有个好点儿的主意,你可以把马卖了。"

"卖野火?你知道我是多么喜欢这匹马!"

"好了,你可以明天骑着它去狩猎会,我知道有几个人想买它,明天他们肯定也在狩猎会,这很容易。"

"不行,明天我没时间去狩猎会。我——我得去参加奥斯古德太太的生日舞会。"

"噢!"邓斯坦大笑起来,"没准儿你能在那儿见到可爱的南茜小姐——你会和她跳舞——你会和她谈情说爱……"

"住嘴!"戈弗雷喊道,他的脸红了。"别这么说南茜小姐,否则我杀了你!"

"别这么生气,哥哥,"邓斯坦冷冷地说,"这是你和她的好机会,真的,我劝你对她好一点儿。咱们都知道莫丽开始喝酒了,有一天她喝多了酒死了,你就能娶南茜了,她不会介意做第二个太太的,如果她根本不知道有个第一个的话。有我这么个好弟弟为你保守秘密,你是多么幸运呀。"

戈弗雷脸色惨白,有些颤抖。"邓斯坦,我受够了,别欺人太甚,或许我会马上去找父亲承认这一切。他早晚会发现真相,因为

hunt *v.* 打猎; *n.* 狩猎会。
push *v.* *press* (*person*) *hard* 逼迫,催逼。**discover** *v.* *find out* 发现。

because Molly says she'll come and tell him. She wants everyone to know we're married. When the Squire knows the truth, you won't get any more money from me!'

Dunstan replied lightly, 'Do what you like, brother.'

Godfrey hesitated. He knew he had fallen into Dunstan's trap, when he made the mistake of marrying Molly. It was Dunstan who had introduced his brother to Molly, hoping that Godfrey would fall in love and marry her. Dunstan was clearly delighted that his evil plan had succeeded. Godfrey was now in a difficult situation. He no longer loved his young wife, and could not stop thinking of Nancy Lammeter. He felt sure that with Nancy as his wife he would not need to have secrets, and could be open and honest with everybody. But for the moment he had to give Dunstan whatever he wanted, keep Molly happy, and lie to his father and his friends. If he told his father the truth, the situation would become impossible. The Squire would disinherit him and he would be just a poor working man for the rest of his life. And far worse than that, he would lose any hope of marrying Nancy. No! He could not accept that. He would find the money for Dunstan, and wait for the situation to get better. Living with fear in his heart, the fear of being discovered, was better than living without Nancy's love.

He turned to Dunstan. 'It's just like you to talk of selling Wildfire—the best horse I've ever had!'

'Let *me* sell him for you—you know I'm good at buying and selling. I can ride him to the hunt for you tomorrow, and

莫丽说会来告诉他。她希望每个人都知道我们结婚了。等父亲知道了,你就别想再从我这儿弄一分钱!”

邓斯坦轻松地回答:“随你便,哥哥。”

戈弗雷犹豫了,他知道自从错误地和莫丽结婚以后,自己就掉进了邓斯坦的陷阱。邓斯坦把戈弗雷介绍给莫丽,就是想让他爱上她并娶她。邓斯坦显然很得意自己的计划能够成功。戈弗雷现在处于困难的境地,他不再爱他的年轻妻子,也不能停止想念南茜·拉默特。他深信如果南茜成为自己的妻子,他就不再需要保守什么秘密,可以诚实、坦率地去面对每一个人。但现在邓斯坦要什么,他就得给什么,必须让莫丽高兴,并且必须对父亲和朋友们撒谎。如果向父亲说出实情,情况将不可想像,自己会被父亲取消继承权,会像一个可怜的工人一样过完下半辈子。更糟糕的是,自己将再不可能娶到南茜了。不,他不会接受这一切!他要给邓斯坦找钱,等待事情好转。怀着怕被发现的恐惧活着,总比得不到南茜的爱活着要强。

他转向邓斯坦。“卖掉野火——我最好的马,这正是你的行径!”

“让我替你去卖——你知道我善做买卖。明天我会把它骑到狩猎会,然后带钱

light *a*. *free from sorrow* 轻松的。**hesitate** *v*. *show indecision* 犹豫。**introduce** *v*. *make known* 介绍。

bring you back the money. But you must decide. You lent me that money, and you'll have to pay it back to the Squire. So it's your problem, not mine!'

Godfrey thought for a moment. 'All right,' he said. 'But make sure you bring me back all the money, Dunstan!'

The next morning, as Dunstan was riding Wildfire out of Raveloe, he passed the old quarry. All the stone had been taken out of it and it was no longer used; now all that was left was a deep hole full of reddish water. Opposite the quarry was Silas Marner's cottage. Dunstan suddenly had an idea. 'Everybody in Raveloe talks of the weaver's money—he must have a lot hidden away in that cottage! Why doesn't Godfrey borrow some money from him, and pay him back when he becomes the Squire?' He wondered whether to go back to the Red House at once, to tell Godfrey about this wonderful idea of his, but he did not want to miss the hunt, so he decided to continue on his way.

At the hunt he met several friends and neighbours, and before the hunt started he managed to sell Wildfire for a good price. The money would be paid when he brought the horse to the neighbour's house later that day. Dunstan knew it would be safer to take the horse there immediately, so that he could be sure of receiving the money. But he was confident that he could take care of Wildfire during the hunt, and so, after a glass or two of whisky, he joined the other riders in the fields. This

回来给你。不过这必须由你来决定。钱你已经借给我了,你得去还给父亲,所以这是你的问题而不是我的。”

戈弗雷想了一会儿。“好吧,”他说,“不过你必须把所有的钱拿回来给我!”

第二天早晨,邓斯坦骑着野火离开瑞福洛时,从老采石场经过。所有的石头都已经被采走,采石场已经废弃多时,现在只剩一个满是红水的大深洞了。西拉斯·马南的草屋就在采石场的对面。邓斯坦忽然有了个主意。“瑞福洛的每个人都在谈论织布匠的钱——他一定在草屋里藏了很多钱。戈弗雷干嘛不向他借点儿,等成了乡绅后再还给他呢?”他犹豫了一下是不是马上回去把自己的好主意告诉戈弗雷,但最后还是决定继续赶路,因为他不想错过狩猎会。

在狩猎会,邓斯坦遇到了几个朋友和邻居,在狩猎会开始前他已经把野火卖了个好价钱,说好晚些时候把马送到邻居家里再拿钱。邓斯坦知道马上把马送去更安全,这样他肯定能拿到钱。但他相信自己在狩猎会上能照料好马。于是,喝了一两杯威士忌后,他加入了其他狩猎者的行列。不幸的

quarry *n. a place where stones, sands, etc. is take out of ground* 采石场。**immediately** *ad. at once* 马上,立刻。

time, however, he was not as lucky as usual, and horse and rider fell while jumping a gate. Dunstan got up, shaken but unhurt, but poor Wildfire's back was broken, and in a few moments he died.

Dunstan looked around, and was glad to see that no other riders had noticed his accident. He did not want people to think he was a bad rider. He did not care much about Wildfire, because he thought he now had a much better plan to offer Godfrey. The worst thing was that he would have to walk home, something he was not at all used to doing.

He drank some more whisky from the bottle he kept in his pocket, and started down the country road. He kept thinking about Silas's money. There would certainly be enough for his own needs as well as Godfrey's. Dunstan thought it would be easy to frighten the weaver a little, and then Silas would quickly agree to lend his money.

It was four o'clock in the afternoon, and the whole countryside was covered by a thick mist. Dunstan did not see anyone on his way back to Raveloe. He knew he was getting close to the old quarry, although he could not see the road in front of him. At last he saw light coming from the weaver's cottage, and he decided to knock at the door. 'Why not ask the old man for the money now?' he thought.

But when he knocked loudly, there was no reply. And when he pushed the door, it opened. Dunstan found himself in front of a bright fire which showed every corner of the small living-

是,这次邓斯坦没有平时幸运,在跳过一个篱笆门时,马和骑手都摔倒了。邓斯坦站了起来,摔得够呛但没伤着,而可怜的野火的背却摔断了,几分钟后,它死了。

邓斯坦看看四周,很高兴没有别的骑手注意到他的事故,他不想让人觉得他是个不好的骑手。他并不在乎野火,因为他觉得他有更好的主意提供给戈弗雷。最麻烦的是他得步行回家了,这可是他一点儿也不习惯的。

又喝了些身上酒瓶里的酒,邓斯坦踏上了回家的乡村小路。他一直在想西拉斯的钱,那些钱肯定够哥哥和自己用的了。邓斯坦相信很容易就能吓住织布匠,让他把钱借出来。

这时是下午 4 点,整个村野都被浓雾笼罩着。邓斯坦在回瑞福洛的路上没有看到一个人。虽然看不见前面的路,但他知道自己已经接近老采石场了。终于看到了织布匠屋里的灯光,他决定去敲门。"为什么不现在就去向老头儿借钱?"他想。

他大声敲门的时候,屋里没有人答应,推了推,门开了。邓斯坦进到了一个被炉火照亮了每一个角落的小屋里,西拉斯·马南

rider *n. person who rides* (*a horse*, *etc.*) 骑手。**unhurt** *a. not hurt* 没有受伤。**offer** *v.* 提供。

room. Silas Marner was not there. Dunstan was tired and cold, so he went quickly to sit by the warm fire. As he sat down, he noticed a small piece of meat cooking over the fire. It was hanging from a large door key.

'So, the old man's cooking meat for his supper, is he?' thought Dunstan. 'But where is he? Why is his door unlocked? Perhaps he went out to fetch some wood for the fire, and fell into the quarry! Perhaps he's dead!' This was an interesting new idea. 'And if he's dead, *who inherits his money? Who would know that anybody had come to take it away?*' And the most important question of all—'*Where is the money?*'

Dunstan's excitement made him forget that the weaver could still be alive. He wanted Silas to be dead, and he wanted Silas's money. He looked round the cottage again. There was very little furniture, just a bed, the loom, three chairs and a table. Dunstan looked under the bed, but the money was not there. Then he noticed a place on the floor, near the loom, where the floorboards looked different. By pulling up one of the boards, he discovered Silas's hiding-place. He took out the two heavy bags filled with gold, put the boards back and hurried to the door.

Outside, the rain was falling heavily, and he could not see anything at all. Carrying the heavy bags, he stepped forward into the darkness.

不在家。邓斯坦觉得又冷又累,赶紧在暖和的炉火前坐下。坐下时,他发现一小片肉吊在一把大钥匙上,在火上烤着。

"这是老家伙为自己烧的晚饭吧!"邓斯坦想,"他去哪儿了?为什么不锁门?也许出去运柴火,结果掉采石场里了!没准他死了!"这是个有趣的新想法。"如果他死了,谁继承他的钱?谁会知道有人来过把钱拿走了?"可更重要的问题是——"钱在哪儿?"

兴奋使邓斯坦忘了织布匠有可能还活着。他希望西拉斯死了,他希望得到西拉斯的钱。于是他重新看看小屋,家具很少,只有一张床、织布机、三把椅子和一张桌子。看看桌子下面,钱不在。邓斯坦注意到织布机旁边地上的一个地方,地板看起来有些特别,扒开一块板,他发现了西拉斯的藏钱之处。他取出两个装满金币的袋子,把板盖好,急忙跑向屋门。

外面的雨下得很大,邓斯坦什么也看不见。拿着沉沉的袋子,他走进黑暗之中。

hang *v. be supported from above so that the lower end is free* 悬挂。**furniture** *n. things needed in a house, such as chairs, tables and beds* 家具。

3
Where is Silas's gold?

When Dunstan Cass left the cottage, Silas Marner was only a hundred metres away. He was walking home from the village, where he had gone to buy what he needed for his next day's work. His legs were tired, but he felt almost happy. He was looking forward to supper-time, when he would bring out his gold. Tonight he had an extra reason to hurry home. He was going to eat hot meat, which was unusual for him. And it would cost him nothing, because someone had given him a piece of meat as a present. He had left it cooking over the fire. The door key was needed to hold it safely in place, but Silas was not at all worried about leaving his gold in the cottage with the door unlocked. He could not imagine that a thief would find his way through the mist, rain and darkness to the little cottage by the quarry.

When he reached his cottage and opened the door, he did not notice that anything was different. He threw off his wet coat, and pushed the meat closer to the fire. As soon as he was warm again, he began to think about his gold. It seemed a long time to wait until after supper, when he usually brought out the coins to look at. So he decided to bring out his gold immediately, while the meat was still cooking.

But when he took up the floorboards near the loom, and saw the empty hole, he did not understand at once. His heart beat

3 西拉斯的金子哪儿去了?

邓斯坦·凯斯离开的时候,西拉斯仅仅在100米之外,他从村里买了第二天干活用的东西,正往家里走。西拉斯的腿很累,但他心里很高兴。他期待着晚饭时间的到来,那时他又可以拿出金子来了。今晚他匆匆回家还有个特别的理由,他今天要吃一块热热的烤肉,平时他很少吃肉。不过他并没有花钱,因为这块肉是别人送给他的礼物。他出来时已经把它烤在了火上,肉是用大门钥匙串起来的,西拉斯一点儿也不担心不锁门而把金币留在小屋里,他不信会有贼能在这样的大雾、大雨里摸黑找到他在采石场边上的小草屋。

他回到家,打开门,没有发现任何异常。他脱下湿衣服,把肉向火上推了推,一暖和过来,他马上开始想他的金子。他不能像平时那样等到吃完晚饭再把金子拿出来,那要等太久了,他决定趁肉还在烤着,马上拿出金子来。

当他扒开织机旁的地板,看到洞里空空的什么也没有时,并没有马上明白过来。他

present *n. gift* 礼物。**unlocked** *a. not fastened with a lock* 未锁的。**mist** *n. water vapor in the air, at or near earth's surface* 薄雾。

violently as his trembling hands felt all round the hole. There was nothing there! He put his hands to his head and tried to think. Had he put his gold in a different place, and forgotten about it? He searched every corner of his small cottage, until he could not pretend to himself any more. He had to accept the truth—his gold had been stolen!

He gave a wild, desperate scream, and stood still for a moment. Then he turned towards his loom, and almost fell into the seat where he always worked. He touched the loom to make sure it, too, had not been stolen. Now he was beginning to think more clearly. 'A thief has been here! If I can find him, he'll have to give back my gold! But I was only away for a short time, and there's no sign of anyone entering the cottage.' He wondered whether it was really a thief who had taken his money, or whether it was the same cruel God who had already destroyed his happiness once. But Silas preferred to suspect a thief, who would perhaps return the money. He began to think it must be Jem Rodney, a local poacher, who had known about Silas's money, and who sometimes visited the cottage. Silas felt stronger now that he thought he knew the thief. 'I must go and tell the Squire, and the police!' he said to himself. 'They'll make Jem give me back the money!' So he hurried out in the rain without a coat, and ran towards the Rainbow.

He thought he would find the most important people in Raveloe at the public house, but in fact most of them were at Mrs

的心剧烈地跳着，用颤抖的手把洞摸了个遍，什么也没有！他用手抱着头，想好好想一想。是不是自己把金子放在了别处又忘了？他找遍了草屋的每一个角落，但终于一无所获，他不能再欺骗自己了。他不得不接受这一事实——他的金子被偷走了！

他发出一声绝望的惨叫，呆呆地站了一会儿，猛地转向织机，险些跌倒在每天干活的座位上。西拉斯摸着织布机以确定他的织布机还没有被偷走。这时他的思想清楚了一些。"一定是有贼来过！如果我能找出这个人，他就得把金子还给我！可我只离开了一会儿，也看不出有人进过屋呀！"他不明白是真的有贼偷走了他的钱，还是那个曾经毁坏过他幸福生活的残忍的上帝又在惩治他。不过西拉斯宁愿怀疑是贼干的，因为贼还可能把钱还回来。他开始猜想贼一定是本地的偷猎者杰姆·罗德尼，因为他知道西拉斯有钱，而且以前来过小屋。西拉斯以为自己知道贼是谁了，就感到自己强大了点儿。"我必须去告诉乡绅和警察！"他对自己说，"他们会让杰姆还我钱。"于是他来不及披外衣就冲进雨里，向彩虹酒馆跑去。

西拉斯本以为一定能在酒馆见到瑞福洛最重要的人们，可实际上大部分人都去参

violently *ad. with great force* 强烈地。**desperate** *a.* (*of a person*) *filled with despair and ready to do anything, regardless of any danger* 绝望的。**suspect** *v. to think that something is true, but not certain* 怀疑。**poacher** *n.* 偷猎者。

Osgood's birthday dance. There were, however, five villagers at the Rainbow, enjoying an interesting conversation about ghosts, while drinking their beer.

'I tell you, people *have* seen ghosts,' the butcher said. 'And I'll tell you where, too. Behind the church!'

'That's right,' agreed old Mr Macey. 'You young ones aren't old enough to remember, but people have seen ghosts near the church since I was a boy. Oh yes, it's true.'

The farrier laughed scornfully. 'Ghosts! People *imagine* they see things on a dark night! You can't make *me* believe in ghosts! It's a question of fact! There are no ghosts!'

'Now, now,' began the landlord, who always tried to keep the peace, 'in some ways you're all wrong, and in some ways you're all right, that's my opinion. There *are* ghosts, and there *aren't*, well, that's what people say. And...'

Just then Silas's white face appeared suddenly in the doorway. He had run all the way from his cottage, so he could not speak for a moment. He stared silently at the men with his strange staring eyes, looking exactly like a ghost. For a few minutes nobody said anything, while Silas tried to control his breathing. Then the landlord spoke.

'What do you want, Master Marner? Come, tell us.'

'Robbed!' cried Silas, suddenly able to speak. 'I've been robbed! I want the police, and the Squire!' He waved his arms wildly as he spoke.

'Hold him, Jem,' said the landlord to the poacher, who was

加奥斯古德太太的生日舞会了。然而还是有5个村民在酒馆中一边喝着啤酒，一边闲谈着有关鬼怪的事。

“告诉你们，有人真的见过鬼，”屠户说，“而且我告诉你们在哪儿，就在教堂后面！”

“没错，”麦西老先生附和着，“你们太小了，不记得，从我小时候起人们就在教堂附近看见过鬼。没错，是真的。”

马掌匠嘲讽地大笑起来。“鬼！人们总幻想着在黑夜里看到什么！你别想让我相信！这是个事实问题！世界上根本没有鬼！”

“行了，行了，”酒馆主人发话了，他总想维持和平，“我觉得你们都不对，又都对，人们总说有鬼没鬼，但……”

这时西拉斯苍白的脸突然出现在过道里。他从草屋一路跑来，所以一时说不出话来，只是不声不响地用那双奇怪的、直瞪着的眼睛盯着人们，确实有点儿像一个鬼。半晌没有人说话，而西拉斯则在努力地使自己呼吸平稳下来。然后酒馆主人打破了沉默。

“怎么了，马南师傅？来，告诉我们。”

“贼！”西拉斯喊道，他忽然能说话了。“我被贼偷了！我要找警察，还有乡绅！”他边说边疯狂地挥着手。

“按住他，杰姆，”酒馆主人对坐在门边

ghost *n. soul of dead person* 鬼魂。**imagine** *v. picture to oneself* 想像。

sitting near the door. 'I think he's gone mad.'

But Jem moved quickly away. 'Not me!' he replied. 'I don't want anything to do with a ghost!'

'Jem Rodney!' cried Silas, turning and staring at the man he suspected.

'Yes, Master Marner?' answered Jem, trembling a little.

'If it was you who stole my money,' said Silas, going close to Jem, 'just give it back to me, and I won't tell the police. Please—just give it back.'

'Stole your money!' cried Jem angrily. 'I'll throw this glass at you if you accuse me of stealing your money!'

'Come now, Master Marner,' said the landlord firmly, taking Silas by the arm. 'You must explain what you mean if you want us to believe you. And sit down by the fire to dry your clothes. You're very wet.'

'That's right,' said the farrier. 'No more staring like a madman. That's what I thought you were at first—not a ghost, of course.'

The weaver sat down, in the centre of the little group of men, and told his story. It felt strange but pleasant to him, to talk to his neighbours and tell them his problems. The men realized at once that Silas was telling the truth. They had suspected him of working for the devil, but they knew now that the devil was no longer taking care of him.

'Well, Master Marner,' said the landlord in the end, 'you mustn't accuse poor Jem. He sometimes steals a chicken, we all

的偷猎者说，"我想他疯了"！

可杰姆马上躲到了一边。"别让我按他，"他答道，"我可不想和魔鬼打交道！"

"杰姆·罗德尼！"西拉斯转脸盯着这个他怀疑的人喊道。

"怎么啦，马南师傅？"杰姆有点儿发抖。

"如果是你偷了我的钱，"西拉斯走近了说，"还给我，我不会去报告警察。请你还给我！"

"偷你的钱！"杰姆生气地喊道，"如果你再诬陷我偷你的钱，我就用杯子砸你！"

"来，马南师傅，"酒馆主人拉住西拉斯坚决地说，"如果想让我们相信你，你必须向我们讲清楚。来，坐下烤烤你的衣服，你都湿透了。"

"对，"马掌匠说，"别再像疯子似地瞪着眼了，我一开始就认为你不是个魔鬼而是个疯子。"

西拉斯坐下来，在一小群人中间讲起自己的故事。和邻居讲话并告诉他们自己的问题，这种感觉让西拉斯感到很奇特，可也很愉快。人们马上意识到西拉斯讲的是实话，他们确实怀疑过西拉斯为魔鬼工作，可他们相信现在魔鬼不再照料他了。

"好了，马南师傅，"酒馆主人最后说，"你千万别再为难可怜的杰姆了，我们都知道他有时会偷只鸡什么的，可今晚他一直在

devil *n. the enemy of God, or a bad, evil person* 魔鬼。**accuse** *v. say that sb. has done wrong* 指责，控告。

know that, but he's been sitting here drinking with us all evening. So he's not the thief.'

'That's right,' said old Mr Macey. 'You can't accuse someone who hasn't done anything wrong, Master Marner.'

These words brought the past back to Silas, and he remembered standing in front of his accusers in the Light Street chapel. He went up to Jem.

'I was wrong,' he said miserably. 'I'm sorry, Jem. I had no reason to accuse you. But—where can my gold be?'

'Perhaps some stranger came to your cottage while you were out,' said the farrier. 'But we must report the robbery to the police and the Squire immediately.'

Next morning, when the whole village heard about the stolen gold, they all discussed it excitedly. A few people still did not trust Silas or believe his story. Most people, however, were suspicious of the pedlar who had visited Raveloe the month before. Perhaps he had returned to hide near the quarry, and steal the money when Silas left his cottage. Several villagers thought they remembered his evil-looking face, and felt sure he was not honest.

Silas himself remembered that the pedlar had come to his cottage door recently. He hoped the pedlar was indeed the thief, because the police could catch him and make him give back the money. His home seemed very empty to him without his gold, and he desperately wanted to get it back.

这儿和我们一起喝酒，所以他不会是贼。”

“没错，”麦西老先生说，“你不能难为没有做错事的人，马南师傅。”

这些话使西拉斯想起了过去的事，想起了许多年前在日光街教堂里他站在指责他的人面前。他走到杰姆面前。

“我错了，”他痛心地说，“对不起，杰姆，我不该难为你，可是——我的金子哪儿去了？”

“可能有陌生人在你不在的时候闯进了你的小屋，”马掌匠说，“但不管怎样我们必须马上向警察和乡绅报案。”

第二天，全村人都听说了丢金子的事，大家都在兴奋地议论，一小部分人仍然不相信西拉斯和他的故事，而大多数人都怀疑上个月来过瑞福洛的小贩，没准儿他溜回来藏在了采石场附近，然后趁西拉斯出门的时候偷了钱。有几个村民更是想起来他们早就从小贩那张罪恶的脸上看出他不是好人。

西拉斯自己也想起小贩不久前到过自己的小屋。他希望小贩真的是贼，那样警察就能抓住他让他还钱了。没有了金子，小屋显得空空荡荡，西拉斯不顾一切地想找回金子。

pedlar *n. a person who goes from house to house selling small articles* 小贩。

4
Godfrey is in trouble

Godfrey was not very surprised to find that Dunstan had not come home after his day's hunting. Perhaps he was staying the night at a public house. But when Dunstan did not return home the next day, Godfrey began to worry about Wildfire. He did not trust his brother, and wondered if Dunstan had gone away to spend the money on gambling. So he decided to go to look for him. On the road near Raveloe he met his neighbour, John Bryce, who had arranged to buy Wildfire from Dunstan.

'Well, Godfrey,' said Bryce, 'did your brother tell you about the horse?'

'What do you mean, John?' replied Godfrey quickly. 'No, he hasn't been home yet. What's happened to my horse?'

'Ah, so he was yours, was he? Dunstan told me you'd *given* him Wildfire. I was going to buy him, you know.'

'What's Dunstan done? Is Wildfire hurt?' asked Godfrey crossly.

'Worse than that,' answered Bryce. 'I'm afraid your horse is dead. We've only just found him. Your brother rode him to the hunt and the horse fell at a gate and broke his back. So you haven't seen Dunstan since yesterday?'

'No, and he'd better not come home now!' replied Godfrey angrily. 'How stupid I was to trust him with my horse!'

4 戈弗雷有麻烦了

戈弗雷对于邓斯坦在狩猎的第二天没有回家来一点儿也不奇怪。他也许又在哪间酒馆呆了一夜。可第三天邓斯坦还没回来，戈弗雷开始有些为他的野火担心了。他信不过他的兄弟，怀疑邓斯坦是不是去把钱花在赌场上了。于是他决定去找邓斯坦，在离瑞福洛不远的路上他遇到了邻居约翰·布莱斯，那个想从邓斯坦那里买走野火的人。

"怎么样，戈弗雷，"布莱斯说，"你弟弟告诉你关于马的事儿了吗？"

"什么意思，约翰？"戈弗雷马上问，"他还没回家。我的马怎么了？"

"噢，那是你的马，是吗？邓斯坦告诉我你把野火给他了，你知道我曾经想买那马。"

"邓斯坦干什么了？野火受伤了？"戈弗雷怒气冲冲地问。

"更糟，"布莱斯回答，"你的马死了，我们刚找到它。你兄弟骑它去狩猎，在跳一个篱笆门的时候马摔断了脊背。从昨天你一直没见你弟弟？"

"没有，他最好别现在回家来！"戈弗雷气急败坏地说，"我太傻了，竟然把马交给他！"

arrange *v. take steps, form plans* 计划，安排。

'But where can Dunstan be? I suppose he wasn't hurt, because we didn't find him near the horse.'

'Him?' said Godfrey bitterly. 'Oh, he'll be all right. He'll never be hurt—he only ever hurts other people! We'll hear of him soon enough, don't worry.'

Bryce said goodbye and rode away. Godfrey rode slowly back into Raveloe, thinking about what he would very soon have to do. There was no longer any escape. He must confess the whole truth to his father. For the rest of the day he planned what he would say. He would explain that he had lent Fowler's money to Dunstan, because Dunstan knew his secret. That would be the right moment to tell the Squire about his secret marriage to Molly. 'But he'll be very angry!' thought Godfrey. 'And when he's angry with people, he just wants to punish them! He won't listen or calm down! But perhaps he'll keep my secret—he's so proud of the family name! And if he disinherited me, everyone would talk about it.'

When he went to bed that night, Godfrey thought he had decided what to say. But when he woke up in the morning, he could not see any reason to confess to the marriage. Why should he lose the chance of marrying Nancy? Why should he tell the whole truth now, when perhaps it was not necessary? No, it would be better to go on in the same way as before. Perhaps Dunstan would stay away for a while, and then there would be no need to tell his father about Molly. 'But today I'll tell the Squire about the money,' he thought. 'He'll have to

“可邓斯坦在哪儿？我想他没事，因为我们在马旁边没找到他。”

“他？”戈弗雷苦涩地说，“他不会有事儿的。他永远不会受伤——他只会去伤别人！你放心，我们很快会听到他的消息。”

布莱斯告别后骑马走了，戈弗雷边骑马慢慢向村里走，边想下面怎么办。没法再逃了，他必须向父亲承认一切。这一天剩下的时间他都在想该向父亲说些什么。他要向父亲解释因为邓斯坦知道他的秘密，所以他不得不把福勒还来的钱借给了邓斯坦，正好趁此机会告诉父亲自己和莫丽的秘密婚姻。“但他会很生气！”戈弗雷想，“他一定会惩罚惹他生气的人！他不会听我说，也不会平静下来！但也许他会保守我的秘密——他是那么珍视家族的荣誉！如果他取消我的继承权，每个人都会议论这件事。”

晚上上床的时候，戈弗雷已经决定了怎么说，可早上起床时，他又怎么也找不到承认秘密婚姻的理由了。为什么要失去娶南茜的机会？真有必要现在就承认一切吗？不，像以前那样过更好。也许邓斯坦会在外面呆一段时间，那也就没必要对父亲讲莫丽的事了。“但今天我得对他讲钱的事，”他想，“他必须知道这件事。”

bitterly *ad. with disappointment and anger* 痛苦地。

know about *that*.'

Godfrey was already in the dining-room when his father arrived for breakfast. The Squire sat down at the head of the table and ordered the servant to bring him some beer.

'Haven't you had breakfast yet, Godfrey?' he asked.

'Yes, I have, sir,' replied Godfrey, 'but I was waiting to speak to you.'

'Well, you young people have plenty of time,' answered the Squire. 'We older ones have to do all the work.'

Godfrey looked straight at his father. 'Sir,' he said bravely, 'I must tell you—something very unfortunate has happened to Wildfire.'

'What! Has he broken a leg? I thought you could ride better than that! Well, you can't expect me to pay for a new horse. I'm very short of money at the moment. And I'm angry with Fowler—he *still* hasn't paid me what he owes me. If he doesn't pay today, he'll go to prison!' The Squire's face was red, and he banged angrily on the table as he spoke.

'It's worse than breaking a leg,' continued Godfrey miserably. 'Wildfire's dead. But I don't want you to buy me another horse. I just feel sorry I can't pay you—you see, sir, the truth is, I'm very sorry, Fowler *did* pay the money. He gave it to me, and I was stupid enough to let Dunstan have it. And he was going to sell Wildfire and then I was going to repay you the money.'

The Squire's face was purple now, and for a moment he

父亲来吃早饭时，戈弗雷已经在餐厅了。乡绅在桌子上首坐下，叫用人拿啤酒来。

“还没吃过早饭吗？戈弗雷？”他问。

“吃过了，先生，”戈弗雷回答，“我等您想说点儿事。”

“你们年轻人总有空闲，”乡绅回答，“可我们老家伙什么活都得干。”

戈弗雷直视着他父亲。“先生，”他鼓足勇气说，“我必须告诉您——野火发生了不幸。”

“什么！它的腿摔断了？我还以为你会骑马呢！别指望我再给你买一匹新马，我这一阵没钱，我正在为福勒生气——他还没有还欠我的钱。今天再不还，我会让他进监狱！”乡绅涨红了脸，生气地拍着桌子说。

“比腿断了更糟，”戈弗雷接着沮丧地说，“野火死了。不过我并不想让您给我买新马，我只是为不能还上您的钱而难过——您看，很抱歉，实际上福勒先生已经还了钱，他还给了我，而我太傻了，竟然把钱交给了邓斯坦，我必须再还给您，所以邓斯坦就去卖野火。”

乡绅的脸已经变成了紫色，气得一时说

servant *n. a person who is paid to work in someone else's house* 仆人。

could not speak. 'You—you let Dunstan have my money? *Why* did you give it to him? And why did he want it? Where's Dunstan now? He'll answer my questions, or leave this house! Go and fetch him at once!'

'Dunstan hasn't come home, sir. The horse was found dead, and nobody knows where Dunstan is.'

'Well, why did you let him have my money? Answer me!' said the Squire, staring angrily at Godfrey.

'Well, sir, I don't know,' replied Godfrey, hesitating. He was not good at lying, and was not prepared for his father's questions.

'You don't know?' the Squire repeated scornfully. 'Well, *I* know why. I think you've done something wrong, and you've bribed Dunstan to keep it a secret! That's it, isn't it?'

The Squire had made a very clever guess, and Godfrey's heart banged in sudden alarm. He was not ready to confess everything yet. 'Well, sir,' he said, trying to speak carelessly, 'it was just a little business between Dunstan and me. You wouldn't be interested in it, you know.'

'How old are you now? Twenty-six?' asked the Squire angrily. 'Old enough to look after your money and mine too! I've been much too generous to you boys, but I'm going to be harder on you all from now on. You've got a weak character, Godfrey, like your poor mother. I think you need a wife who knows what she wants, because you can't decide anything by yourself! When you were thinking of marrying Nancy

不上话来。“你——你把我的钱给了邓斯坦？为什么给他？他为什么要钱？邓斯坦现在在哪儿？他必须回答我的问题，否则就滚出这幢房子！马上去给我找他！”

“邓斯坦还没回家来，先生，马被找到时已经死了，没人知道邓斯坦在哪儿。”

“那你为什么把我的钱给他？回答我！”乡绅愤怒地盯着戈弗雷。

“我也不知道，先生。”戈弗雷犹豫地回答，他不善于说谎，对父亲的提问也没有准备。

“你不知道？”乡绅藐视地重复道。“我知道了，一定是你做了错事要邓斯坦为你保密！对不对？”

乡绅做了一个聪明的猜想，戈弗雷心里一惊。他还没有准备对父亲承认一切。“噢，先生，”他尽量轻描淡写地说，“这只是我和邓斯坦之间的一点儿小事儿，您不会感兴趣。”

“你多大了？26？”乡绅生气地问，“你已经足够大了，应该能照看你的钱和我的钱了！我以前对你们太宽容了，可从现在开始我会对你们严厉起来。你的性格太软弱了，戈弗雷，就像你那可怜的妈妈。我想你需要有个头脑清楚的老婆来帮帮你，你自己根本不会做任何决定！我不是同意你娶南西·拉

fetch *v. go for and bring back* 接来，叫来。**scornful** *a. showing the feeling that someone is bad, stupid, weak, etc.* 轻蔑地。**guess** *v. give an answer based on supposition* 猜想。

Lammeter, I agreed, didn't I? Have you asked her or not? She hasn't refused to marry you, has she?'

'No, I haven't asked her,' said Godfrey, feeling very hot and uncomfortable, 'but I don't think she'll accept me.'

'Don't be stupid, Godfrey!' said the Squire with a scornful laugh. 'Any woman would want to marry into our family! Do you *want* to marry her?'

'There's no other woman I want to marry,' said Godfrey, avoiding his father's eyes.

'Well, then, let me speak to her father for you, since you aren't brave enough to do it yourself. She's a pretty girl, and intelligent.'

'No, sir, please don't say anything at the moment,' said Godfrey quickly. 'I must ask her myself.'

'Well, ask her then. When you marry her, you'll have to forget about horses and so on. It'll be good for you to do some serious work. You should get married soon.'

'Please don't try to hurry things, sir,' begged Godfrey.

'I'll do what I like,' said the Squire firmly. 'And if you don't do what I want, I'll disinherit you and you can leave the house. Now, if you know where Dunstan's hiding—I expect you do—tell him he needn't come home. He'll pay for his own food from now on.'

'I don't know where he is, sir. Anyway, it's *you* who should tell him to leave home.'

'Don't argue with me, Godfrey,' said the Squire, turning

默特吗？有没有向她求婚？她没有拒绝你吧？”

“我还没有问她，”戈弗雷感到一阵燥热，很不自在，“不过我认为她不会接受。”

“别傻了，戈弗雷！”乡绅嘲笑他说，“所有女人都希望嫁到咱们家！你想不想娶她？”

“除了她，我谁都不想娶，”戈弗雷不肯看父亲的眼睛。

“好吧，既然你没有勇气自己讲，那我替你对她父亲说。那是个漂亮姑娘，也很聪明。”

“不，先生，请先别说，”戈弗雷赶紧说，“我必须自己对她说。”

“那好，去对她说吧。娶了她以后，你必须忘了那些马什么的。做些正经事对你有好处。你应该赶快结婚。”

“请您别急，先生。”戈弗雷请求父亲。

“我想怎样就怎样，”乡绅坚决地说，“如果你不按我想的去做，我将取消你的继承权，你可以离开这里。现在，如果你知道邓斯坦在哪儿——我想你知道——去告诉他，他不用再回来了。从现在起，他得自己付饭钱了。”

“我不知道他在哪儿，先生。不管怎样，只有您才可以对他说让他离开这个家。”

“别跟我争论，戈弗雷，”乡绅的注意力

avoid *v. keep away, escape* 避免。**intelligent** *a. smart, clever* 聪明的。

back to his breakfast. 'Just go and tell the servants to get my horse ready.'

Godfrey left the room. He was relieved that his father had not discovered the whole truth. However, he was a little worried that the Squire would try to arrange his marriage with Nancy. While he was married to Molly, he could not marry Nancy, although it was his dearest wish. But as usual he was waiting and hoping for some unexpected change in his situation, which would save him from any unpleasantness.

转回他的早餐，"去让用人把我的马备好。"

戈弗雷离开餐厅，他为父亲没有发现全部实情长出一口气。可是，他有些担心父亲会为他安排和南茜的婚事。虽然娶南茜是他最热切的愿望，但他不可能既娶莫丽，又娶南茜。不过，像往常一样，他等待并希望着会发生一些意想不到的变化，把自己从所有这些麻烦中解脱出来。

argue *v. give reason in support of one's position and against other's position* 争论。**relieve** *v. give (sb.) a feeling that a problem has gone away* 放松。

5
Silas's neighbours

In the weeks following the robbery, the police tried hard to find the pedlar, because so many people suspected him of being the thief. But there was no sign of him in any of the towns and villages round Raveloe.

Nobody was surprised at Dunstan Cass's absence. Once before he had stayed away for six weeks and then come back. Nobody imagined he could have anything to do with the robbery. The villagers continued to discuss Silas and his lost gold, but they had no more explanations to offer.

Silas himself still had his loom and his work, so he went on weaving. But the only thing that had made his life worth living had gone, and now he had nothing to look forward to. A lifetime of empty evenings lay ahead of him. He did not enjoy thinking of the money he would earn, because it reminded him of the money he had lost. As he sat weaving, he sometimes used to moan quietly to himself. And in the evenings, as he sat alone in front of the fire, he used to put his head in his hands and moan again.

But this disaster had one good result. Little by little, Silas's neighbours realized it was wrong to be suspicious of him. He was just a poor, simple, harmless man, who needed their help. They showed their new opinion of him in many different ways. Some of the women, who were baking cakes and

5 西拉斯的邻居们

失窃案后的几周里，因为那么多人都怀疑那个小贩是贼，警察就费了很大劲查找他，但是在瑞福洛周围的村子和镇子里都找不到他的踪影。

没有人对邓斯坦·凯斯的失踪表示奇怪，以前有一次他曾离家6周以后才回来。没人想到他会和失窃案有关。村民们仍在谈论西拉斯和他丢了的金子，可人们都找不到更新的解释。

至于西拉斯本人，他还有他的织布机和他的工作，所以他继续织布。可是生活中唯一有价值的东西失去了，他不再有什么可期望的了。今后的一生将只有空虚的夜晚。他不再喜欢去想将要挣到的钱，那会使他想起丢失的钱。坐着干活的时候，他有时会对自己呻吟。晚上，一个人坐在炉火前，他也常会用手抱着头痛苦地呻吟。

不过他的灾难也有一个好的结果。慢慢地，邻居们认识到以前对西拉斯的怀疑是不对的。他只是一个穷困、简单、无恶意的人，需要他们的帮助。他们通过许多不同的方式表达对马南的新看法。有的妇女会在

moan *v. to make a long, sad sound to show that someone is unhappy* 呻吟。

preparing meat for Christmas, brought him presents of food. Some of the men, who had nothing to give him, stopped him in the village to ask about his health, or visited him to discuss the robbery. They often finished their conversation by saying cheerfully, 'Now you're the same as the rest of us—we're poor too! Cheer up, Master Marner! If you get ill and can't work any more, the Squire'll give you food and your neighbours will take care of you.' This did not make Silas feel better, but he realized it was meant kindly.

Old Mr Macey, the church clerk, came to the cottage one day, to explain how his opinion of the weaver had changed.

'You see, Master Marner,' he said in his high old voice, 'I used to think you worked for the devil—you've always looked strange, you know. But now I'm sure you're not evil, just a little bit crazy. That's what I tell the neighbours.'

He stopped to give Silas time to reply, but the weaver did not speak. He was sitting with his head in his hands as usual. He knew that the old man was trying to be kind, but he was too miserable to show any interest.

'Come, Master Marner, what's your answer to that?' asked Mr Macey, a little impatiently.

'Oh,' said Silas, slowly lifting his head, 'thank you. Thank you for your kindness.'

'That's all right,' replied the old man, pleased. 'Now, you shouldn't sit here moaning, you know. Here's my advice to you. Ask Tookey in the village to make you a Sunday suit—I

准备圣诞晚餐或者烤面包时送给他一些食物，那些没什么可给他的男人也会在村里叫住他问候他或者到小屋来看他，和他聊关于失窃案的事。谈话结束的时候他们通常会愉快地说："现在你和我们这些人一样了——我们也是穷人！高兴起来，马南师傅！如果你病了，不能再工作了，乡绅会给你食物，邻居们会照顾你。"这些虽然不能让西拉斯感觉好受些，但他知道这是好意。

有一天，执事老麦西先生到小屋来解释他对于织布匠看法的改变。

"你知道，马南师傅，"他用苍老的高音说，"我以前以为你为魔鬼工作——你知道你老是看起来怪怪的。可现在我肯定你不邪恶，只是有一点儿古怪，我就是这么对邻居们讲的。"

他停下来等西拉斯回答，可西拉斯没有出声，只是像平常一样用手抱着头坐着，他知道这个老人在试图表示友好，不过他实在是太沮丧了，没有兴趣。

"怎么样，马南师傅，你对我说的怎么看？"麦西先生有点儿不耐烦了。

"噢，"西拉斯慢慢抬起头，"谢谢你，谢谢你的好意。"

"没什么，"老头儿高兴了，"我看你不应该再坐在这儿呻吟了。听听我的意见吧。去找村里的图齐给你做一件礼拜服——我

cheerfully *ad*. *happily* 高兴地。**realize** *v*. *understand* 意识到。**impatiently** *ad*. *not with patience* 不耐烦地。

don't expect you've got one—and then you can come to church with your neighbours. It'll make you feel better. You're not an old man yet, although you look like one. How old were you when you came here first? Twenty-five?'

'I don't remember,' answered Silas, shaking his head.

That evening, Mr Macey told a number of villagers at the Rainbow, 'Poor Master Marner doesn't know how old he is! And I don't suppose he knows what day of the week it is! He really is a bit crazy.'

Another villager, Dolly Winthrop, was also worried about Silas's absence from church. She was a large, fresh-faced woman with a sweet, patient smile, who was always busy from early morning until late at night, and who went to church herself every Sunday. She believed in helping her neighbours, and if someone in Raveloe was ill or dying, Dolly was often asked to take care of the patient. This good, sensible woman decided that Silas needed her help. So one Sunday afternoon she took her son Aaron, a pretty little boy of seven, to visit the weaver. As they came closer to the cottage, they heard the sound of the loom.

'Oh dear! Working on a Sunday! That's bad!' said Mrs Winthrop sadly. She had to knock loudly on the door before Silas heard. He said nothing, but opened the door to let them in, and Dolly sat down in an armchair.

'I was baking yesterday, Master Marner,' she said, 'and I've brought you some of my cakes. Here they are.'

想你一定没有礼拜服——然后和邻居一块儿到教堂来。这样你会好受些。你虽然看着像个老头,可实际上不老。你到这儿时多大? 25?”

“我不记得了。”西拉斯摇着头回答。

这天晚上,麦西先生在酒馆对好多村民宣布:“可怜的马南师傅竟然不知道自己多大! 我想他也不会知道今天星期几! 他真是有点儿疯。”

另一个村民多莉·温思罗普也在为西拉斯不去教堂而担心。这是个气色很好的高大女人,有着温柔、耐心的笑容。她每天从清早忙到深夜,每周日必到教堂礼拜。她把帮助邻居当作自己的责任,村里有人生病或生命垂危,人们总是请她去看护病人。这位善良、聪明的女人觉得西拉斯需要她的帮助,于是,一个礼拜天的下午,多莉带着7岁的儿子阿荣,一个漂亮的小家伙,来看望织布匠。走近小屋,他们听到织布机的声音。

“天哪! 礼拜日还工作! 这可不好。”温思罗普太太难过地说。她使劲敲门,西拉斯才能听到。他默默地开门让客人进来,多莉坐到一把扶手椅里。

“我昨天烤了面包,马南师傅,”她说,“今天给你带了些来。喏。”

patient *a. having patience* 耐心的。**sensible** *a. having or showing good sense* 聪明的,明白事理的。

'Thank you,' replied Silas, taking the little bag of cakes Dolly was holding out to him. Aaron was hiding behind his mother's chair, in childish fear of the weaver.

'You didn't hear the church bells this morning, perhaps, Master Marner?' Dolly asked gently. 'This cottage is a long way from the village.'

'Yes, I heard them,' answered Silas. For him Sunday bells did not mean anything. There had been no bells at the Light Street chapel.

'Oh!' said Dolly. 'But—but do you *have* to work on a Sunday? You could make Sunday different from the other days, you know, by washing yourself, and cooking a little piece of meat, and going to church. And Master Marner, Christmas Day will be here soon! If you put on your best clothes and go to church and see the flowers and hear the singing, you'll feel much better! You'll know there is Someone you can trust!'

Dolly did not usually talk so much, but the matter seemed extremely important to her.

'No, no,' Silas replied. 'I don't know anything about church. I've never been to church.'

'Never been!' repeated Dolly. 'Were there no churches in the town you were born in?'

'Oh yes,' said Silas, 'there were a lot of churches. It was a big town, you see. But I only ever went to chapel.'

Dolly did not understand this word, but was afraid of asking any more questions, in case 'chapel' meant something evil. After

“谢谢你!”西拉斯接过多莉递给他的袋子。阿荣躲在妈妈的椅子后面,他还有些害怕织布匠。

“你今天早晨或许没听到教堂的钟声,马南师傅?”多莉轻轻地问,“这个小屋离村里太远了。”

“我听见了,”西拉斯回答,礼拜日的钟声对他没有任何含意,日光街小教堂没钟。

“噢!”多莉说,“可——可你一定要在礼拜日工作吗?你可以把礼拜日搞得和平时不同一些,你也知道,可以洗洗澡,烤块肉,然后上教堂去。而且马南师傅,马上要到圣诞节了!如果穿上最好的衣服到教堂去看看花,听听歌,你会感觉好多了!你会知道那里有你可以信赖的人!”

多莉平时话并不多,可这事对她很重要。

“不,不,”西拉斯回答,“我不懂教堂的事,我从没去过教堂。”

“从没去过!”多莉重复道,“你出生的城镇没有教堂吗?”

“有,”西拉斯回答,“有很多教堂,因为那是个大镇子,可我只去小教堂。”

多莉不懂这个词,可又不敢再多问,她生怕这个“小教堂”与魔鬼有关。仔细想了

childish *a. of a child* 孩子般的,孩子的。**bell** *n.* 钟(声)。**extreme** *of the highest degree* 极端的。

considering carefully for a moment, she said, 'Well, Master Marner, it's never too late to start going to church. It's very pleasant listening to the singing and the good words. If we go to church, then when trouble comes, Someone will take care of us. And if we do our best, then I believe Someone will help us when we need help.'

Dolly's explanation of her simple religion did not seem at all clear to Silas, but he did understand that she was asking him to go to church. He did not want to agree to that. Just then young Aaron came out from behind his mother's chair, and Silas offered him one of Dolly's cakes.

'Oh Aaron!' said his mother. 'You're always eating! No, don't give him any more, Master Marner. But he can sing a song for you. I'm sure you'll like it. It's a beautiful Christmas carol. Come, Aaron, let's hear it.'

Little Aaron stood up straight and sang his carol in a clear, sweet voice. Dolly listened with delight, hoping that the carol would help to persuade Silas to come to church.

'You see, Master Marner,' she said when Aaron had finished, '*that's* Christmas music. The Christmas Day service is wonderful, with all the voices and the music. I hope you'll be there with us. And remember, if you feel ill, I'll be happy to come and cook or clean for you. But I beg you, please stop weaving on Sundays. It's bad for soul and body, I'm sure. We must go now. Goodbye, Master Marner.'

'Thank you, and goodbye,' said Silas, as he opened the door

一会儿,她说:"马南师傅,什么时候开始上教堂都不算晚,听圣歌和赞美诗的感觉好极了。如果我们经常做礼拜,在有困难的时候,就会有人来帮助我们。只要我们尽力去做,我相信我们会在需要的时候得到帮助的。"

虽然听不太懂多莉对自己简单信仰的解释,可西拉斯知道她在劝说自己去教堂。但他不想照着去做。正在这时阿荣从妈妈的椅子后面出来了,西拉斯给了他一块多莉做的蛋糕。

"嗨,阿荣!"他妈妈叫道,"你总在吃!不,马南师傅,别再给他了。不过他可以给你唱首歌,我想你会喜欢,这是一首圣诞颂歌。来,阿荣,唱给我们听听。"

小阿荣站直了,开始用清晰、甜美的声音唱他的颂歌。多莉高兴地听着,希望歌声能有助于劝说西拉斯去教堂。

"你看,马南师傅,"阿荣唱完她说,"这就是圣诞音乐,圣诞节的礼拜仪式棒极了,有各种声音和音乐。我希望你和我们一起在教堂。记住,如果你不舒服,我很乐意来替你做饭,打扫,但我请求你不要在礼拜日工作。我肯定这对灵魂和肉体都有害。我们得走了。再见,马南师傅。"

"谢谢你,再见。"西拉斯为他们打开门。

consider *v. think about* 考虑。**religion** *n.* 宗教。**carol** *n. a song usually sung at Christmas* 颂歌。**persuade** *v. cause to believe* 说服。

for them. He could not help feeling relieved when she had gone. Now he could weave and moan as much as he liked.

Mr Macey and Dolly had tried hard to persuade Silas to go to church. But in the end he spent Christmas Day alone in his cottage, looking out at the cold grey sky. In the evening, snow began to fall, and he felt more distant and separate from his neighbours than ever. He sat in his robbed home, moaning miserably to himself, not noticing that his fire was no longer burning and that he was getting cold.

But in Raveloe the church bells were ringing and the church was fuller than all through the rest of the year. It was a special day for everybody, and after the service they all hurried home in the biting cold to eat and drink with their families.

At the Red House nobody spoke of Dunstan's absence. The village doctor, Dr Kimble, and his wife were guests there for Christmas lunch, and the day passed happily.

The servants, however, were already preparing for the New Year's Eve dance which Squire Cass gave every year. It was the best party of the year, and guests used to come from miles around. Godfrey was looking forward to this year's party more than usual. But he was still worried.

'What if Dunstan returns?' he thought. 'He'll tell the Squire about my secret marriage! And Molly's asking for more money! I'll have to sell something for cash. But on New Year's Eve, I can forget everything for an evening, and sit with Nancy, and look into her eyes, and dance with her...'

客人走后他不禁感到很轻松,因为他又可以织布,可以想怎么呻吟就怎么呻吟了。

麦西先生和多莉尽了很大努力想劝西拉斯去教堂,可圣诞日西拉斯还是一个人留在了小屋里,望着窗外冷冷的灰色天空。晚上,开始下雪了,他感到跟邻居们距离更远,更孤独了。他坐在被偷过的家里,对自己痛苦地呻吟着,没注意到火炉里的火已经熄了,自己也越来越冷。

此时,瑞福洛的教堂的钟声在响,教堂里比平时任何时候人都多。对每个人这都是特别的一天,仪式完毕人们都在刺骨的寒冷中匆匆赶回家和家人一起吃喝庆祝。

红屋里没人提起邓斯坦的缺席。乡村医生金布尔先生和他太太被请来一起吃午饭,这一天过得很愉快。

用人们已经开始准备乡绅凯斯每年主办的新年夜舞会了。这是一年中最好的晚会,方圆几里地的客人都会来。戈弗雷比往年都更盼着新年晚会。可他也有一点儿担心。

"邓斯坦回来怎么办?"他想,"他会向父亲告发我的秘密婚姻!莫丽又在要更多的钱!我将不得不卖些东西换钱。不过新年之夜我可以暂时忘掉这一切,我要坐在南茜旁边,看着她的眼睛,和她跳舞……"

distant *a. far apart* 遥远的。**separate** *a. physically disconnected* 分离的,不相连的。

6
The New Year's Eve dance

On December 31st it was snowing and very cold. All day there were ladies and gentlemen arriving at the Red House.

Godfrey Cass was waiting at the door for the only guest he cared about, Nancy Lammeter. Finally she arrived, sitting behind her father on his horse, looking more beautiful than ever. Her lovely face blushed as she saw Godfrey come forward to lift her down from the horse. 'Why is he waiting for me?' she thought. 'I thought I made it clear to him that I'll never marry him. People say he leads a bad life, and I can't marry a man like that.'

But the Squire appeared just then, to welcome his guests, and in the excitement nobody noticed Nancy's pink face as Godfrey's strong arms lifted her down. She hurried into the house with the other ladies to change her clothes.

The house was full of servants running here and there. Mrs Kimble, who always helped the Squire arrange these parties, was giving orders in a loud voice. Cooks were preparing food in the kitchens, and there was already a wonderful smell of baking in the air.

Upstairs, the ladies were excitedly putting on their best dresses, while talking to each other all the time. Nancy met her aunt, Mrs Osgood, who introduced her to some visitors of hers.

6 新年舞会

虽然12月31日的天气很冷，而且下着雪，可一整天都有人从四面八方到红屋来。

戈弗雷在门口等待着他唯一关心的客人——南茜·拉默特。终于她来了，坐在马背上，在他爸爸背后，比平时更美丽动人。当戈弗雷过来扶她下马的时候，南茜漂亮的脸一下子红了。“他等我干什么？”她想，“我想我已经清楚地告诉过他我不会嫁给他。人们说他生活糜烂，我可不会嫁给这样的人。”

这时乡绅出来迎接他的客人，人们都很高兴，也就没人注意到戈弗雷用强壮的手臂扶她下来时她的红脸。南茜和其他女子一块儿跑进屋里去换衣服。

屋里用人们在跑这儿跑那儿地服务，金布尔太太在大声下达着命令，她经常帮乡绅安排这些聚会。厨子们在厨房忙着准备饭菜，空气里飘着烤面包的香味。

楼上，女士们一边不停地聊天一边换上最漂亮的衣服。南茜遇到了姨妈奥斯古德太太，姨妈把自己的客人介绍给她，其中有

blush *v. become red in the face* 脸红。**pink** *n. a color of pale red* 粉红色。**welcome** *v. greet on arrival* 欢迎，迎接。

The Misses Gunn were two young ladies who were not beautiful, but dressed very fashionably.

Just then Nancy's older sister Priscilla arrived. She was a large, cheerful girl, with a round face and a nose pink with cold. As they were changing their clothes, Priscilla said to Mrs Osgood, 'Look at our dresses, aunt! Of course Nancy looks beautiful in hers, but this colour makes *me* look yellow! Nancy says we must wear the same dresses, because we're sisters, although I'm five years older! I'm ugly, I know I am. But I don't mind!' She turned to Mrs Osgood's two visitors. 'In my opinion the pretty girls are useful—I'm sure you agree—to catch the men. I don't think men are worth worrying about. Any woman with a good father and a good home had better stay single. That's what I'm going to do, anyway. We ugly girls don't need husbands!'

Mrs Osgood stood up and said quickly, 'My visitors and I should go downstairs now. Priscilla and Nancy, we'll see you later.' And the three ladies hurried out.

'Oh really, Priscilla!' cried Nancy, when they were alone. 'You never think before you speak! I'm sure the Misses Gunn thought you were very impolite! You almost told them they were ugly!'

'Did I?' asked Priscilla in surprise. 'Well, that's the way I am. I always tell the truth. But *I'm* the ugly one—just look at me!'

'Priscilla, you know I asked *you* to choose the dresses,'

两位年轻女士，甘氏姐妹，她们不太漂亮但穿得很时髦。

这时南茜的姐姐普丽西拉来了，她是个快活的圆脸大个子女孩，鼻子冻得红红的。换衣服时，普丽西拉对奥斯古德太太说："看我们的衣服，姨妈，南茜穿起来当然漂亮，可我穿起来太老了！南茜说我们是姐妹，要穿一样的衣服，尽管我比她大5岁！我知道我丑，可是我不在乎。"她又转向姨妈的两个朋友，"我想你们也同意女孩子漂亮就容易抓住男人的心，我可不在乎男人。有个好爸爸、好家庭的女人最好单身。我就打算这样。我们丑姑娘不需要丈夫。"

奥斯古德太太赶紧站起来说："我们要下楼了。普丽西拉，南茜，过会儿见。"3个女人急匆匆出去了。

"真是的，普丽西拉！"只剩她们姐妹俩时南茜生气地说，"你从来不在讲话前先想想！我敢肯定甘氏姐妹认为你很无礼！你差不多是在告诉她们她们是丑姑娘！"

"是吗？"普丽西拉很奇怪，"嗨，我这人就这样，我总是讲实话。可是看看我，我也丑呀！"

"普丽西拉，你知道我是让你来挑的衣

fashionably *ad. in a fashionable manner* 时髦地。**catch** *v. attract the attention of sb.* 吸引。**impolite** *a. not polite* 不礼貌的。

replied Nancy worriedly. 'I don't mind what colour I wear.'

'You look lovely in this colour, dear child! You know you always have whatever you want in the end, although you never give orders or shout about it. I'm looking forward to seeing you married. It'll be fun watching you make your husband do exactly what you want.'

'Don't say that,' answered Nancy, blushing. 'You know I'm never going to get married.'

Priscilla laughed. '*I'm* the one who'll stay single. And if you don't like Godfrey Cass, well, there are plenty of other young men. Come, let's go downstairs now.'

Although Priscilla was right in saying she was not good-looking, she was very popular among her neighbours because she was so cheerful and sensible. And Nancy was not only considered to be the most beautiful girl in and around Raveloe, but also one of the most intelligent.

Seats at the dining-table had been kept for the Lammeter sisters. Priscilla was taken to sit between her father and the Squire. Nancy felt herself blushing again as Godfrey Cass came to lead her to a seat between himself and the vicar, Mr Crackenthorp. She knew that if she married Godfrey, she would one day be the most important woman in Raveloe, the Squire's wife. But she repeated firmly to herself that she could not marry a man of bad character.

As she sat down, the vicar, who was always polite to ladies, said with a smile, 'Ah, Miss Nancy, you're looking lovely this

服，"南茜为难地说，"我不在乎穿什么颜色。"

"傻孩子，你穿这种颜色好看！虽然你从不会大嚷大叫或者发号施令，可你最后总能得到你想要的。我盼着看到你结婚，看着你让你的丈夫按你的意思去做，多开心呀！"

"别说这些，"南茜的脸红了，"你知道我永远不会结婚。"

普丽西拉笑了，"我才是那个要单身的女人，如果你不喜欢戈弗雷·凯斯，还有很多别的小伙子。走吧，咱们下楼去！"

虽然普丽西拉确实像她说的那样，不太好看，可她在邻居中人缘很好，因为她开朗而且懂事。而南茜不仅是瑞福洛一带最漂亮的女孩，而且也是最聪明的女孩。

餐桌边拉默特姐妹的座位已经留好了，普丽西拉的座位在爸爸和乡绅之间。南茜觉得自己又脸红了，她被戈弗雷领到了他自己与教区牧师克拉肯索普先生之间的座位上。她知道如果嫁给戈弗雷，自己就会成为瑞福洛最显贵的女人，乡绅的妻子。可她反复对自己强调不能嫁给一个品行不端的人。

她坐下时，一贯对女士彬彬有礼的牧师微笑着说："啊，南茜小姐，您今晚真漂亮，

popular *a.* *well-liked by people* 受欢迎的。**vicar** *n.* *a priest in the Church of England* 教区牧师。**character** *n.* 品格，性格。

evening. Isn't she, Godfrey?'

Godfrey made no reply, and avoided looking at Nancy. There was too much he wanted to say to her. But the Squire, who always enjoyed his parties and was feeling extremely cheerful, was rather impatient with his son. He thought *he* had better speak, if Godfrey was too shy to do it himself.

'That's right,' the Squire said loudly. 'When I look at Miss Nancy here, I think she's more beautiful than any girl I've ever seen.'

While they were eating and drinking, people around the table were listening with interest to the Squire's words. 'Perhaps Godfrey will marry Nancy after all!' the vicar's wife whispered to Mrs Osgood. Mr Lammeter's back was very straight as he looked across the table at his daughter. He was a serious, careful gentleman, who considered the Lammeters a better family than the Casses. He had already decided that Godfrey must change his way of life before Nancy could possibly marry him.

Just then Dr Kimble called across the table, 'Miss Nancy, will you save a dance for me?'

'Come, come, Kimble,' said the Squire, 'let the young ones enjoy themselves. My son Godfrey'll be angry if you take Miss Nancy away. I expect he's asked her for the first dance already. Haven't you, Godfrey?'

Godfrey was feeling very uncomfortable by now. Turning to Nancy, he said as lightly as possible, 'I haven't asked her yet,

是不是,戈弗雷?"

戈弗雷没有回答,也尽量不去看南茜。他有太多的话想对她说。可这时对晚会心满意足的乡绅对自己的儿子有些不耐烦了。他认为既然儿子太害羞张不开嘴,那么自己最好亲自说了。

"是的,"乡绅大声说,"我觉得南茜比我见过的任何姑娘都要漂亮。"

桌上所有的人都在一边用餐一边饶有兴趣地听着乡绅的话。"大概戈弗雷还是会娶南茜!"牧师的太太小声对奥斯古德太太说。拉默特先生在桌子对面笔直地坐着,看着女儿。这是一位严肃谨慎的绅士,他认为拉默特家比凯斯家还要好。他早就决定在戈弗雷痛改前非之前不会把南茜嫁给戈弗雷。

这时金布尔先生隔着桌子对南茜发出了邀请:"南茜小姐,可不可以和我跳支舞?"

"行了,金布尔,"乡绅插了进来,"让年轻人玩他们的吧!你把南茜小姐带走,我儿子戈弗雷会生气的。我想他已经邀请南茜小姐和他跳第一支舞了,是不是戈弗雷?"

戈弗雷感到很不自在,他转向南茜,尽量小声地说:"我还没有,可我希望她同意,如

whisper *v. speak in a very low voice* 耳语,轻声细语。

but I hope she'll agree, if nobody's asked her...'

'No, I haven't accepted anyone else,' replied Nancy quietly with a blush.

'So will you please have the first dance with me?' asked Godfrey, beginning to feel better. She had not refused him!

'I will,' answered Nancy coldly. She was still sure she would not marry him, but she wanted to remain polite.

'Ah well, you're a lucky man, Godfrey,' said Dr Kimble with a laugh. 'I think I can hear the music starting now!'

The guests got up from the table in pairs and small groups, to move into the large hall, where the dancing was about to start. The small village band was already playing, as the Squire led the vicar's wife to the end of the hall to start the dance. They were followed by Godfrey and Nancy, and the other ladies and gentlemen.

As the dance went on, Godfrey felt happier and happier. Holding Nancy in his arms, he forgot all his problems. Suddenly the Squire's heavy foot stood on part of Nancy's dress, and some of the material was pulled away at the waist. Nancy asked Godfrey to take her to a quieter place, where she could repair the damage. He took her to a small room near the hall, hoping they would have a few private moments together. But Nancy sat down on the chair furthest away from him, and said coldly, 'Thank you, sir. You needn't stay. I'm very sorry about taking you away from the dance.'

'It's not very kind of you,' said Godfrey, moving close to

果还没人请她的话……”

“不，我还没接受任何人的邀请。”南茜轻声回答，脸又一红。

“那你能否和我跳第一支舞？”戈弗雷的感觉好了一点儿。她没有拒绝自己！

“可以。”南茜冷淡地回答。虽然仍然肯定自己不会嫁给他，可南茜想尽量保持礼貌。

“好呀，你是个幸运的小子，戈弗雷。”金布尔先生笑着说，“我想已经开始奏乐了！”

客人们一对对或三五成群地起身走到大厅里，舞会要开始了。在乡村小乐队的伴奏下，乡绅把牧师的太太领到大厅的尽头带头跳起来，接下来是戈弗雷和南茜，然后是其他客人们。

跳着舞，戈弗雷感到越来越幸福。搂着南茜，他忘掉了一切烦恼。忽然乡绅的脚重重地踩住了南茜的长裙，把衣服腰间的部分扯坏了。南茜让戈弗雷带她到一个清静的地方去整理衣服。戈弗雷把她带进了大厅旁边的一间小屋，希望他们能够有一段单独相处的时间。可南茜坐在了离他最远的椅子上，冷冷地说：“谢谢您，先生，您不必呆在这儿，很抱歉让您从舞会上出来。”

“这样可不太好，”戈弗雷走近她一点

private *a. belonging to one person or a group of people* 私下的，属于个人的。**furthest** *a. situated at the longest distance* 最远的。**waist** *n.* 腰，腰部。

her, 'to be sorry you've danced with me.'

'I didn't mean that!' replied Nancy, blushing prettily. 'Gentlemen have so many things to enjoy. I'm sure one dance can't matter very much.'

'You know that isn't true. You know one dance with you means more to me than anything else in the world.'

Nancy was a little surprised. Godfrey had not said anything like this to her for a long time. She replied firmly, 'I'm afraid I can't believe you, Mr Godfrey.'

'Nancy, if I changed my life, would you think better of me? Would you—like me, then?' Godfrey knew these were dangerous words, but the sudden chance of speaking to her alone made him say more than he had planned.

'I'd be glad to see a good change in anybody, sir.'

'You're very hard, Nancy,' said Godfrey bitterly. 'You could help me to be better. I'm very miserable—but *you* don't feel anything.'

'I think *people who behave badly* don't feel anything,' said Nancy sharply, forgetting to be cool and distant.

Godfrey was delighted. He wanted to make her argue with him, to show him that she cared about him. But just then Priscilla hurried in, saying, 'Dear child, let me look at your dress! I saw the Squire step on it during the dance.'

'I suppose I'd better go now,' Godfrey said disappointedly to Priscilla.

'It doesn't matter at all to me whether you go or stay,' said

儿，说，“你为什么不愿意和我跳舞呢？”

“我不是这个意思！”南茜的脸红得很可爱，“绅士们有那么多事可做，我肯定跳支舞没什么重要。”

“你知道不是这样的，你知道和你跳一支舞对我比任何事都重要。”

南茜有些吃惊，戈弗雷很久没有对她说这样的话了。她坚决地回答：“戈弗雷先生，我恐怕不能相信你。”

“南茜，如果我改变我的生活，你会觉得我好一点儿吗？你会——喜欢我吗？”戈弗雷知道这些话很危险，可这突然来的单独谈话的机会使他讲了比计划里多得多的话。

“我对任何人的好的变化都感到很高兴，先生。”

“你太苛刻了，南茜。”戈弗雷有些苦涩，“你可以帮我变好。我很痛苦——可你什么也感觉不到。”

“我认为品行不端的人才会什么也感觉不到。”南茜尖锐地说，忘了冷静和距离。

戈弗雷很高兴，他想让南茜和他争论，这说明南茜仍然在乎他。可这时普丽西拉闯了进来，说：“好孩子，让我看看你的衣服，我看见乡绅在跳舞的时候踩到你了。”

“我想我得走了。”戈弗雷失望地对普丽西拉说。

“你走不走我都无所谓。”普丽西拉不耐

sharp *a*. *harsh*, *severe* 严厉的，尖锐的。

Priscilla impatiently, looking closely at the waist of Nancy's dress.

'Do *you* want me to go?' Godfrey asked Nancy.

'Do whatever you like,' replied Nancy, trying to sound cold again.

'Well, I want to stay,' answered Godfrey, and sat down. Tonight he wanted to enjoy being with Nancy for as long as possible, without thinking about what would happen tomorrow.

烦地说,她在仔细地看南茜衣服的腰部。

"你想让我走吗?"戈弗雷问南茜。

"随你便。"南茜尽可能恢复以前的冷淡。

"那么我想留下来。"戈弗雷说着坐下来。他今天晚上要尽可能多地呆在南茜身边,不管明天会怎么样。

7
Silas finds his 'gold'

But while Godfrey Cass was managing to forget his problems by the lovely Nancy's side, his wife was walking with slow, uncertain steps along the snow-covered road to Raveloe. She was carrying her sleeping child in her arms.

For some time now she had planned to come to Raveloe on New Year's Eve. She knew that her husband would be at the centre of a happy, smiling group of friends, and she had chosen this moment to appear in front of all his family and guests at the Red House dance. 'I don't care if Godfrey is ashamed of me!' she thought bitterly. 'I want people to know we're married!' Sometimes she hated her husband, because he was still handsome, and had money, while she was no longer pretty, and very poor. She blamed him for her miserable life, but in her heart she knew she should blame her drinking. It had become a habit with her to spend most of the money Godfrey gave her on gin. She had a bottle in her pocket now, which she had lifted to her lips several times during her journey.

It was already seven o'clock in the evening, and there was a freezing wind. Molly did not know she was very near Raveloe. Her legs were tired and the gin was beginning to make her feel sleepy. She thought she would rest for a while, and, still holding her child, she lay down on the snow. She did not notice that the ground was cold.

7 西拉斯找到了他的“金子”

就在戈弗雷·凯斯坐在可爱的南茜身边试图忘记一切烦恼的时候，他的妻子正在大雪覆盖的道路上艰难地向瑞福洛的方向跋涉着。她的孩子睡在她的臂弯里。

她已经计划好要在新年之夜到瑞福洛去，她知道她的丈夫一定正在被幸福欢笑的朋友们环绕着，她就是要选择这个时候出现在他的家人和朋友们面前，出现在红屋的舞会上。“我不在乎戈弗雷会以我为耻，”她苦涩地想，“我要让大家知道我们结婚了！”有时她恨她的丈夫，因为他仍然英俊而且富有，可她已经不再漂亮了，而且贫困。她为自己的不幸怨他，但在心底里她知道应该怨自己酗酒。她已经习惯于把戈弗雷给她的钱用来买酒，现在她兜里就有一瓶酒，而且一路上她已经喝了几次。

已经是晚上7点了，风冷得刺骨。莫丽不知道她已经离瑞福洛很近了。她的腿开始发沉，酒精也开始使她昏昏欲睡。她想应该歇一会儿，于是就抱着孩子，躺到了雪地上。她没有注意地上是那么冷。

uncertain *a*. *easy to change* 易变的。**freezing** *a*. *extremely cold* 冻结的，极冷的。

In a few moments the child woke up, crying, 'Mummy!' But the mother did not seem to hear. Suddenly, as the child fell gently out of its mother's arms on to the soft snow, it noticed a bright, dancing light on the white ground. Interested, the child stood up to see where the brightness came from, and followed the light to an open door, the door of Silas Marner's cottage. The little one toddled right in through the door and sat down by the bright fire. After a few minutes the child felt pleasantly warm, and fell asleep.

But where was Silas while this was happening? In the evenings he sometimes used to open his door and look out. He had some idea that his money would come back, or that someone would come with information about the thief. Tonight was New Year's Eve, and the villagers had told him to stay awake until midnight, because it would bring him good luck if he saw the beginning of the new year. So tonight he was more restless than usual. He opened his door several times during the evening, and stared out, but he saw and heard nothing in the silent, freezing night. The last time, as he was standing at the door, he had one of his fits, and stood there completely unconscious, holding the door open.

When he became conscious again, he closed the door and turned back to the fire. But when his shortsighted eyes looked at the floor in front of the fire, he seemed to see gold there! Gold — his own gold — taken and then brought back to him in the same strange way! His heart beat excitedly, and for a

一会儿孩子醒了,开始哭着喊妈妈。可妈妈好像没有听见。孩子从妈妈的臂中滑落到松软的雪地上时,忽然看到白白的雪地上跳动着一点小小的亮光。出于好奇,孩子站起来想看看光是从哪儿来的。向着亮光,孩子走进了一扇开着的门,这是西拉斯·马南的小草屋。小家伙蹒跚着直进门里走到明亮的炉火前坐下。没过几分钟,孩子暖和过来,甜甜地睡着了。

这时西拉斯在哪儿呢?他晚上有时会打开门看看外面,总觉得有一天他的金子会回来,或者什么人会给他带来关于贼的消息。今晚是新年夜,村里人告诉他今天午夜前不要睡觉,因为看着新的一年到来会给人带来好运。所以今晚他比平时更坐立不安。他几次打开门向外面看,可是在这个静静的寒冷的冬夜,他什么也看不见,什么也听不见。最后一次站到门口的时候,他又犯病了,站在那儿完全失去了知觉。门开着。

恢复知觉以后,他关上门回到炉火前,但当他的近视眼看到炉前的地板时,他好像发现了金子!金子——他的金子——奇怪地离他而去又以同样的方式奇怪地回到了他的身边!他的心剧烈地跳动起来,好一会儿

dancing *a*. *moving in a lively way* 欢快地跳动的。**toddle** *v*. *walk with short unsteady steps* 蹒跚行走。**information** *n*. *knowledge*, *news* 消息。**restless** *a*. *uneasy*, *agitated* 焦躁不安的。

few moments he was unable to move. At last he reached out his hand to touch the gold, but instead of hard, metal coins his fingers felt soft, warm curls.

With great surprise Silas fell on his knees to look at this wonderful thing. It was a sleeping child. Was he dreaming? Could it be his little sister, who had died when he was a child himself? If it wasn't a dream, how had the child entered the cottage? But thinking of his sister made him remember the past, and his life at the Light Street chapel. He wondered if this child was some kind of message from his past, sent perhaps by the God he had once trusted.

Just then the child woke up, and began to cry. Silas held it in his arms, and spoke softly to quieten it. He remembered that he had made some porridge earlier, and gave a little to the child to eat. She stopped crying, and lifted her blue eyes with a smile to Silas's face as she ate. But then she pulled at her wet shoes, trying to take them off, and Silas suddenly realized she had come to the cottage through the snow. So he picked her up and went to the door. As he opened it and went out into the dark, the child cried 'Mummy!' and reached forward, almost jumping out of his arms. A few steps away, Silas found a young woman's body, half-covered with snow.

At the Red House, everybody was enjoying the party. Some people were still eating, while others were dancing or playing cards. Godfrey was looking forward to his next dance with

他都不能移动。终于他伸手去摸那金子,可是没有摸到硬硬的金币,却摸到了软软的暖暖的鬈发。

西拉斯惊奇地跪到地上去看这神奇的东西。这是一个熟睡着的孩子。是不是在做梦?这是不是自己小时候死去的小妹妹?如果不是梦,这孩子怎么到屋里来的?想到妹妹使他想到了自己的过去,想到在日光街小教堂的事。他怀疑这孩子会不会是那他曾经信任过的上帝派来向他传递关于他过去生活的什么信息的。

这时候孩子醒了,开始哭。西拉斯把孩子抱在怀里,轻声地哄着。他想起来自己做的麦片粥,就拿出来喂孩子。孩子不再哭了,一边吃一边抬起蓝眼睛看着西拉斯的脸甜甜地笑。当她使劲想把那双湿湿的鞋子拽掉时,西拉斯想到她一定是从雪里走来的,于是就抱着孩子走向屋门。他打开门走进黑暗中时,孩子喊着妈妈向前挣去,险些从西拉斯的胳膊里跳到地上。几步之外,西拉斯看见一个半埋在雪里的年轻女人。

在红屋里,人们在尽情享受着晚会的快乐,有的人还在吃着东西,有的人在玩纸牌或者跳舞。戈弗雷在等着和南西的下一个

curl *n*. 鬈发。**quieten** *v*. *make quiet* 使安静。**porridge** *n*. 粥,麦片粥。**pull** *v*. *draw* 拉。

Nancy. He was watching her dreamily across the room, when suddenly he saw something that made his lips go white and his whole body tremble. It was his own child, carried in Silas Marner's arms. The weaver had come straight into the hall, where the dancing was going on.

Several people turned to look at the strange figure in the doorway. The Squire could not understand why Silas had come in uninvited. He stood up and asked angrily, 'Marner, what are you doing here?'

'I've come for the doctor,' replied Silas hurriedly. 'There's a woman — dead, I think — near my cottage.'

Godfrey had one great fear at that moment, that the woman was *not* dead. If she were his wife, and she were dead, he would be free to marry Nancy!

While the Squire was calling for Dr Kimble, the ladies came closer to look at the pretty child.

'Whose child is it?' one of them asked.

'I don't know,' replied Godfrey wildly. 'Some poor woman's — she's been found in the snow, I think.'

'You'd better leave the poor child here with us then, Master Marner,' offered Mrs Kimble kindly.

'No — I can't let it go,' said Silas unexpectedly. 'It's come to me — I don't know where from — I want to keep it!'

'Well!' said Mrs Kimble, surprised. 'A single man like you! Take care of a child! Well!' But the little one was holding on

舞。正当他如醉如痴地远远地看着南茜的时候,眼前的景象使他一下嘴唇煞白,浑身发抖。他看到了他的孩子,在西拉斯的怀里。织布匠径直闯进了正在开舞会的大厅。

有人转过去看门口这个奇怪的人,乡绅不明白西拉斯为什么会没有得到邀请就来到晚会上。他站起来生气地问:"马南,你来干什么?"

"我来找大夫,"西拉斯着急地回答,"有个女人在我小屋旁边,我想已经死了。"

戈弗雷这时真怕那个女人没有死,如果那是他的妻子,而且死了,他就可以娶南茜了!

乡绅叫金布尔大夫的时候,女人们都围过来看这个漂亮的小女孩。

"这是谁的孩子?"有人问。

"我不知道,"戈弗雷暴躁地回答,"一个穷女人的——我想是在雪地上发现的那个。"

"你最好把这个可怜的孩子留在我们这儿,马南师傅。"金布尔太太好心地说。

"不——我不让她离开我,"西拉斯的回答出人意料,"她是来找我的,我要留下她,虽然我不知道她从哪儿来。"

"你?"金布尔太太很诧异,"你这么个单身男人!照顾一个孩子!行吗?"可这时候小

hall *n.* *large room for meeting* 大厅。**wildly** *ad.* *madly* 狂暴地。**unexpected** *a.* *not expected* 出乎意料的。

to Silas, and smiling up at him confidently.

Dr Kimble hurried into the hall. 'Where is this poor woman? Near the old quarry? Someone had better fetch Dolly Winthrop. I'll need her to help me.'

'I'll go!' cried Godfrey. He wanted to get away, before anyone noticed his white face and shaking hands, and he needed time to think. He ran out into the night.

When he and Dolly arrived at the quarry, the doctor had moved the woman into Silas's cottage, and Godfrey had to wait outside. He walked up and down in the snow, for what seemed like hours. He knew he should tell the truth about the woman and the child, but he could not make himself do what he knew was right. 'Is she dead?' the voice inside his head asked. 'If she is, I can marry Nancy. And then I'll be good, and have no more secrets. And I'll make sure the child is taken care of, of course.'

When Dr Kimble came out of the cottage, Godfrey tried to speak calmly. 'I thought I'd wait to see...' he began.

'Oh, there was no need for you to come. Why didn't you send one of the men to fetch Dolly? The woman's dead, I'm afraid. She's very thin, and looks very poor. But she's got a wedding ring on. She'll be buried tomorrow.'

'I'll just have a look at her,' said Godfrey quickly. 'I think I saw a woman on the road yesterday with a child. Perhaps it was her.' And he ran into the cottage.

There on the bed was his unloved wife. He only looked at

家伙正靠在西拉斯身上，在信任地对着西拉斯笑。

金布尔大夫跑进大厅："那可怜的女人在哪儿？在采石场附近吗？最好去叫一下多莉·温思罗普，我需要她的帮助。"

"我去！"戈弗雷喊。趁人们还没发现他苍白的嘴唇和颤抖的手，他想赶快离开，他需要时间仔细想想。他一溜烟跑进黑夜中。

当他和多莉到采石场的时候，大夫已经把女人移到了西拉斯的小屋。戈弗雷得在外面等着。他在外面走来走去，觉得大概过了几个小时。他知道他应当讲出关于女人和孩子的实情，可他怎么也不能让自己去做应当做的事。"她死了吗？"他的脑子里有个声音在问。"如果她死了，我就能娶南茜了，我一定要变好，不再做见不得人的事，而且我一定会好好照料孩子的，一定会。"

金布尔大夫出来的时候，戈弗雷尽可能平静地说："我想我应当等在这儿看看……"

"噢，你不必亲自来，怎么不派别人去接多莉？我想那女人已经死了。她很瘦弱，看来很穷，却戴着个结婚戒指。明天给她下葬。"

"我得看她一眼，"戈弗雷很快地说，"我昨天在路上看见了一个抱孩子的女人，也许就是她。"说着他跑进了小屋。

床上躺着他已经不再爱的妻子。他只

confident *a. trusting, fully assured* 有信心的。**bury** *v. place (a dead body) in the ground* 埋葬。

her for a moment, but for the rest of his life he never forgot her sad, tired face.

The weaver had come back with the doctor, and was sitting by the fire, with the child on his knees. The little one was awake, but her wide open blue eyes looked up into Godfrey's face without recognizing him at all. The father was glad of this, but also a little sad, especially when he saw the small hand pull lovingly at the weaver's grey hair.

'So, who's going to take care of the child?' Godfrey asked, pretending not to show much interest.

'*I* am,' replied Silas firmly. 'The mother's dead, and I suppose the child hasn't got a father. She's alone in the world, and so am I. My money's gone, I don't know where, and she's come, I don't know where from. I don't understand it at all, but I'm going to keep her.'

'Poor little thing!' said Godfrey. 'Let me give you something for her clothes.' He put his hand in his pocket and gave Silas some coins.

As he walked back to the Red House, he felt very relieved. Nobody would recognize his dead wife, and soon his secret would be buried with her. Now he could talk of love to Nancy. He could promise to be a good husband to her. Only Dunstan knew about the secret marriage, and perhaps Dunstan would never come home. 'What a good thing I didn't confess everything to the Squire!' he thought. 'Now I can make Nancy and myself happy. And the child? Well, it won't matter to her

看了她一会儿,但终生都没有忘记她那张忧伤疲惫的脸。

织布匠是和大夫一起回来的,他坐在火炉旁,抱着孩子。小家伙醒着,她睁大了蓝眼睛盯着戈弗雷的脸看,可是根本没认出他来。这使父亲很高兴,可也有些难受,特别是当他看到那双小手在充满爱意地拉着织布匠的灰色头发的时候。

"那谁来照料这孩子呢?"戈弗雷努力掩饰自己的关心。

"我,"西拉斯坚决地说,"她妈妈死了,我想孩子也没有爸爸,她像我一样在这个世上孤苦零丁。我的钱不知到哪儿去了,而她不知从哪儿来了。这一切我都不明白,可我一定要抚养她。"

"可怜的小东西!给你些钱去给她买衣服。"戈弗雷从兜里拿出一些钱交给西拉斯。

回红屋的路上,戈弗雷异常轻松,没有人会认识他死去的妻子,他的秘密很快就要和她一起被埋掉了。现在他可以和南茜谈情说爱了,他可以向她保证做一个好丈夫。只有邓斯坦知道那段秘密婚姻,可他可能永远不会再回来了。"我没有向父亲坦白一切是多么对呀!"他想,"现在我可以让自己和南茜幸福了。可孩子呢?嗨,我是不是她父

especially *ad. in particular* 特别地。**pretend** *v. make oneself seem* 假装。**suppose** *v. guess* 猜想,料想。

whether I'm her father or not.'

That week the dead woman was buried in Raveloe, and the child stayed at the weaver's cottage. The villagers were very surprised that Silas had decided to keep her, but they liked him for wanting to help an orphan. The women, especially, were very ready to give him useful advice on taking care of children.

Dolly Winthrop came every day to help Silas. 'It's no trouble,' she said. 'I get up early, so I've got plenty of time. And I can bring you some of Aaron's old baby clothes, so you won't need to spend a lot of money on the child. I can wash her, and give her food, and—'

'Ye—es,' said Silas, hesitating. He was looking a little jealously at the baby in Dolly's arms. 'That's very kind of you. But — but I want to do everything for her myself! I want her to be fond of *me*! She's *my* child!'

'Don't worry,' said Dolly gently, giving him the child. 'Look, she loves you the best. See, she's smiling at you!'

And so Silas learnt how to take care of the little girl. He called her Eppie, which had been his little sister's name. His life was quite different now. When he was working and living only for his gold, he had not been interested in the world outside his cottage, or the people he sometimes met. But now that he had another reason for living, he had to look outward. He spent hours in the fields with Eppie, happily rediscovering the plants he used to know so well. Together they visited his neighbours,

亲对她也并不重要。”

那个星期这个死去的女人被埋在了瑞福洛，小女孩留在了织布匠的小屋。大家很惊讶西拉斯决定收留这孩子，可又都很高兴他能关心孤儿。女人们更是时刻准备着向西拉斯提供抚养孩子的经验。

多莉·温思罗普每天来帮助西拉斯。“没问题，”她说，“我起得早，所以有足够的时间。我可以把阿荣的旧衣服拿来，你也就不必为孩子花很多钱。我可以给她洗澡，可以给她喂饭，可以……”

“好——吧，”西拉斯犹豫地说。他有点儿忌妒地看着多莉怀里的孩子。“你真好，可——我想自己来为她做一切！我想让她喜欢我！她是我的孩子。”

“别担心，”多莉把孩子交还给西拉斯，温柔地说，“看，她最爱的人还是你。看见了吗，她在对你笑呢！”

于是西拉斯学会了照顾这个小女孩。他管她叫埃比，这是他的小妹妹的名字。他的生活全变了。当他为金子而工作而生活的时候，他对屋外的世界，对那些偶然见到的人们毫无兴趣。现在生活的目的变了，他不得不开始看看外面的世界。他花几个小时陪埃比在地里玩，又愉快地重新发现了那些他曾经熟悉过的植物。他们一起去串

orphan *n. a child whose parents are both dead* 孤儿。**jealous** *a. showing a feeling of fear or ill will because of possible loss* 嫉妒的。

who were always delighted to see him and his adopted child. His days and evenings were full, taking care of a trusting, loving child.

Godfrey Cass watched the little girl growing up with great interest. During Eppie's childhood he often gave money to Silas to spend on her, but was careful that nobody should suspect him of being her father. His life was also changing. There was a new firmness about him which everyone noticed. He was looking forward to marrying Nancy very soon. 'Nancy and I will have children!' he thought happily. 'But I won't forget that other child!'

门,去看那些喜欢见到他和他的养女的邻居们。照看这个信赖他、喜欢他的孩子使他的日日夜夜变得很充实。

戈弗雷·凯斯关注地看着小女孩一点儿一点儿长大。埃比小的时候他经常送钱给西拉斯去给埃比买东西,可他又很小心,怕别人怀疑自己是孩子的父亲。他的生活也变了。每个人都能发现他变得稳重了。他盼着能快些娶南茜。"南茜和我会再有孩子。"他高兴地想。"不过我不会忘了那另一个孩子。"

adopt *v. take another person's child into one's own family to become one's own child* 收养。

8
Eppie has grown up

It was a bright autumn Sunday, sixteen years after Silas had found Eppie in his cottage. The Raveloe church bells were ringing, and people were coming out of church after the morning service. First came the new squire, Godfrey Cass, looking a little heavier now, but with a straight back and a firm step. On his arm was his wife Nancy, still a pretty woman. Just behind them came Mr Lammeter and Priscilla. They all went into the Red House.

'You and Priscilla will stay for tea, won't you?' Nancy asked her father.

'My dear, you must ask Priscilla,' replied Mr Lammeter with a smile. 'She manages me and the farm as well.'

'Well, it's better for your health if *I* manage everything, father,' said Priscilla. 'Then there's nothing for you to worry about. No, Nancy dear, we must go home now. But you and I can have a walk round the garden while the servants are getting the horses ready.'

When the sisters were alone in the garden, Priscilla said, 'My dear, I'm very glad you're going to have a dairy. Making your own butter will give you something to think about all the time. You'll never be sad when you've got a dairy.' And she put her arm through her sister's.

'Dear Priscilla,' said Nancy gratefully. 'I'm only ever sad

8 埃比长大了

这是西拉斯在小屋找到埃比 16 年后的秋天的一个晴朗的礼拜日。瑞福洛教堂的钟声响了，做完晨祷的人们陆续走出教堂。走在最前面的是新的乡绅戈弗雷·凯斯，他比以前胖了一些，可是背很直，步伐也很坚定。他的太太南茜挽着他的胳膊。南茜仍然那么漂亮。在他们后面的是拉默特先生和普丽西拉。大家一起走进了红屋。

"你和普丽西拉会在这儿喝茶吧？"南茜问自己的父亲。

"亲爱的，那得问问普丽西拉，"拉默特先生笑着说，"她既管着农场，也管着我。"

"一切由我来管对你有好处，爸爸。"普丽西拉说，"这样你就不用为各种事操心了。不，亲爱的南茜，我们得回家去了。不过咱们可以趁用人备马的时候到花园里去走一走。"

姐妹两人单独在花园里的时候，普丽西拉说："我亲爱的，我真高兴你就要有牛奶厂了。自己做奶酪，你就会整天有事可想了。有了牛奶厂，你就再不会发愁了。"她挽起妹妹的胳膊。

"亲爱的普丽西拉，"南茜感激地说，"只

manage *v.* *handle*, *take control of* 管理。**dairy** *n.* 牛奶厂。

when Godfrey is. I could be happy if *he* could accept our life as it is. But it's more difficult for a man.'

'Men!' cried Priscilla impatiently. 'They're always wanting something new! Never happy with what they've got! I'm glad I was too ugly to get married! I'm much happier with father!'

'Oh Priscilla,' said Nancy. 'Don't be angry with Godfrey—he's a very good husband. But of course he's disappointed that we haven't had children—he wanted them so much.'

'Well, father is waiting for me—I'd better go now. Goodbye, my dear.' And the sisters kissed goodbye.

When Priscilla and her father had left, Godfrey said, 'Nancy, I think I'll just go and look at some of the fields we're draining near the old quarry.'

'You'll be back by tea-time, dear?'

'Oh yes, I'll be back in an hour.'

This was a habit of Godfrey's on Sunday afternoons. He enjoyed walking round the fields that belonged to him now. So Nancy often had a quiet hour at about this time, which she spent reading, or sometimes just thinking.

She remembered all the little things that had happened to her, especially during her marriage, in the last fifteen years. The great sadness of her married life had been the death of her only baby. Like most women, she had looked forward to becoming a mother very much. But when the baby died soon after it was born, she made herself accept the fact. She did not

有戈弗雷发愁的时候我才会发愁。如果他能接受我们的生活，我会很高兴，可这对一个男人来说太难了。”

“男人！”普丽西拉不耐烦地说，“他们总想要新鲜的东西，从不会对得到的东西感到满意！我真幸运太丑了嫁不出去！我和爸爸在一起要快乐得多。”

“哦，普丽西拉，”南茜说，“你别怪戈弗雷——他是个很好的丈夫。当然他因为我们没有孩子失望——他太想要孩子了。”

“好了，爸爸在等我——我得走了。再见，亲爱的！”姐妹俩互相吻别。

普丽西拉和她父亲走后，戈弗雷说：“南茜，我想我得去看看那几片靠近采石场的正在排水的地。”

“你会回来喝茶吗？亲爱的？”

“会，我一小时后回来。”

这是戈弗雷在礼拜日下午的习惯，他喜欢绕着那些现在属于他的土地走一走。南茜会利用这安静的一小时看看书，或是想想事。

她记得以前发生过的所有小事，尤其是结婚15年来的情形。唯一的孩子的夭折是她婚姻生活中最大的痛苦。和大部分女人一样，她渴望着做一个母亲，但她的孩子降生后不久就死了，于是她强迫自己接受了这

drain *v. to make land become dry by causing the water to run off it* 排去……的水。

allow herself to think about it, or to wish for anything different. Godfrey, however, had been terribly disappointed, especially when it seemed likely that Nancy could have no more children.

Nancy's religion was extremely important to her. She firmly believed that people should accept whatever happened to them in life, because it was God who decided everything. But she understood how difficult it was for Godfrey to accept that their marriage would be childless. 'Was I right,' she wondered for the hundredth time, 'to refuse him, when he said we should adopt a child? I believe that if God hasn't given us a child, it's because God doesn't want us to have one. I'm sure I'm right. But poor Godfrey! It's worse for him than for me. I've got him, and the house, and now the dairy to think about. But although he's always good to me, I know he's unhappy—he wants children so much!'

From the first moment Godfrey had spoken of adopting a child, he had mentioned Eppie's name. She had always been the child he wanted to adopt. He had no idea that Silas would rather die than lose Eppie, and he imagined that the weaver would be glad if the child were adopted by the Cass family. 'After all, the girl will have a much better life with us,' he told himself. 'I can't be really happy if we don't have a child. And I can never tell Nancy the truth about Eppie—I'm afraid she'll hate me for it.'

While Nancy was sitting quietly in the Red House, thinking

个事实。她不许自己去想这件事，也不许自己去做其他的设想。然而戈弗雷极其失望，尤其当看到南茜很可能不能再要孩子的时候。

宗教信仰对南茜非常重要，她坚信人们应当接受命运赋予他们的一切，因为那是上帝安排的，但她知道戈弗雷是多么难以接受他们没有孩子的婚姻。“我这样对吗？”南茜第100次问自己，“拒绝按他说的去收养一个孩子？我想上帝没给我们孩子是因为他不想让我们有孩子。我想我是对的。可是可怜的戈弗雷，他比我要痛苦，我拥有了他，拥有了房子，又将有牛奶厂，可他虽然对我一直很好，可我知道他并不开心——他太想要孩子了。”

戈弗雷第一次提起收养孩子的时候就讲到了埃比的名字。他一直很想收养她，没有想到西拉斯宁可死也不愿意失去埃比，只认为织布匠会为埃比被凯斯家收养而高兴。“不管怎样，小姑娘跟着我们会过得好得多。”他对自己说。“没有孩子我不会真的幸福。可我又不能说出关于埃比的实情——南茜一定会因此而恨我的。”

南茜静静地坐在家里想着她丈夫的时

childless *a. without a child* 没有孩子的。**mention** *v. talk about, refer to* 提到。

about her husband, Silas and Eppie were sitting outside their cottage near the quarry. They had been to church too, which they did every week, like the Casses and most of the villagers. Silas had started taking Eppie to church when she was very young, because Dolly Winthrop had persuaded him that every child should have some religious training. Because of Eppie, Silas was completely accepted in Raveloe now. Nobody thought he was strange any more; in fact, he was almost a popular figure in the village.

He was older now, and could not work as hard as he used to. Recently, as he had more time to think, he had begun to remember the past, and his old friends at the Light Street chapel. He realized how his once lonely life had changed since Eppie had come to him. Now he had friends, and trusted people, and was happy. And he began to see that the God in the Raveloe church was the same God he had been so angry with, the last time he had been to the chapel. It seemed to him that there had been some mistake in his past, which had thrown a dark shadow over his early life. Perhaps now he would never know whether Mr Paston, the chapel minister, still thought he was guilty of stealing. And he would never discover why the drawing of the lots had seemed to prove his guilt. 'But there must be a God of goodness in this world,' he thought, 'because He sent Eppie to me. I must just trust, and believe that He is right.'

He had told Eppie how her mother had died in the snow, and

候，西拉斯和埃比正坐在他们采石场旁边的小屋前面。像平时一样。他们也同凯斯一家和其他村民一道做了礼拜。因为多莉劝西拉斯说每个孩子都应该接受宗教教育，所以西拉斯在埃比很小的时候就开始带她去教堂。由于埃比的原因，西拉斯现在完完全全被瑞福洛的人们所接受了。没人再认为他奇怪，实际上，他几乎成了瑞福洛村里一个很受欢迎的人。

西拉斯年龄大了，不能像原来那样拚命干活了。最近，因为有了更多的思考的时间，他开始回忆过去，回忆日光街小教堂的老朋友们。他意识到了自己一度寂寞的生活是怎么因为埃比而改变的。他现在有朋友，信任别人而且幸福。他开始觉得瑞福洛的这个上帝和最后一次去日光街小教堂时他曾气恼过的那个上帝是同一个上帝。他认为自己可能前世做过什么错事，给自己的前半生罩上了一层阴影。可能他永远无法知道小教堂的牧师帕斯通先生是不是仍认为他犯了偷窃罪，他也永远无法发现为什么抽签会证明他有罪。“但这世上一定有一个好的上帝，”他想，“因为他把埃比送给了我。我必须相信他是对的。”

他对埃比讲了她母亲是怎么死在雪地

figure *n*. *person* 人物。
shadow *n*. *area of shade, or dark shape* 影子，暗影。
guilty *a*. 有罪的。

he had given her the dead woman's wedding ring. Eppie was not at all interested in who her real father was, as she thought she had the best father in the world already. At the moment she was sitting close to Silas outside their door in the sunshine. Neither of them had spoken for a while.

'Father,' she said gently, 'if I get married, do you think I should wear my mother's ring?'

'Oh, Eppie!' said Silas, surprised. 'Are you thinking of getting married, then?'

'Well, Aaron was talking to me about it,' replied Eppie, blushing. 'You know he's nearly twenty-four now, and is earning good money, and he'd like to marry soon.'

'And who would he like to marry?' asked Silas with rather a sad smile.

'Why, me, of course, daddy!' said Eppie, laughing and kissing her father. 'He won't want to marry anyone else!'

'And you'd like to marry him, would you?' asked Silas.

'Yes, one day. I don't know when. Aaron says everyone's married some time. But I told him that's not true, because *you* haven't ever been married, have you, daddy?'

'No, child,' said Silas. 'I was a lonely man before you were sent to me.'

'But you'll never be lonely again, father,' said Eppie lovingly. 'That's what Aaron said. He doesn't want to take me away from you. He wants us all to live together, and he'll do all the work, and you needn't work at all, father. He'll be like a son

上的，并把她妈妈的结婚戒指给了她。埃比一点儿也不关心她的亲生父亲是谁，因为她觉得自己已经有了一个世界上最好的爸爸。这会儿她正紧挨着西拉斯坐在门外晒太阳。两人都沉默了一会儿。

"爸爸，"埃比轻声说，"如果我结婚，我要不要戴妈妈的戒指？"

"什么，埃比，"西拉斯吓了一跳，"你想结婚了吗？"

"阿荣对我谈起了，"埃比的脸红了，"你知道他都快二十四岁了，而且也挣钱了，他想早点儿结婚。"

"他想娶谁？"西拉斯笑得很悲伤。

"当然是我了，爸爸！"埃比笑着吻了她的父亲，"他除了我谁也不娶。"

"你想嫁给他，是吗？"西拉斯问。

"是的，有一天会的。我也不知道会是哪一天。阿荣说人总要结婚，我说那可不一定，你就没结过婚，对吧，爸爸？"

"是的，孩子，"西拉斯说，"在你来到我身边之前，我一直是一个孤独的人。"

"不过你不会再孤独了，爸爸，"埃比深情地说，"阿荣也这么说，他不想把我从你身边夺走，他想我们大家生活在一起，他干所有的活儿，你不用再工作了，他会像儿子那样孝敬你。"

lovingly *ad*. *with love* 喜爱地，充满爱意地，深情地。

to you.'

'Well, my child, you're young to be married,' said Silas. 'But he's a good young man. We'll ask his mother what we should do. She always gives us good advice. You see, Eppie, I'm getting older, and I'd like to think of you with a strong young husband to take care of you for the rest of your life. Yes, we'll ask Dolly Winthrop for her opinion.'

"可是,我的孩子,你太小了还不该结婚,"西拉斯说,"可他确实是个好小伙子。咱们问问他妈妈,看看该怎么做。她总能帮我们。你看,埃比,我老了,我也希望你有个年轻强壮的丈夫来照顾你以后的生活。好吧,我们去问问多莉·温思罗普的意见。"

opinion *n. what one thinks on a particular question* 看法,观点。

9
Godfrey confesses at last

At the Red House Nancy was waiting patiently for Godfrey to come home to tea. Suddenly one of the servants ran into the sitting-room, crying excitedly, 'Madam, there are lots of people in the street! They're all running the same way, towards the quarry! Perhaps there's been an accident!'

'Jane, don't get so excited,' replied Nancy calmly. 'I expect it's nothing serious. Go and get the tea ready. Mr Godfrey will be back soon.' But secretly she was saying to herself, 'I hope nothing's happened to Godfrey!'

So when he came into the room, a few minutes later, she was very relieved. 'My dear, I'm so thankful you've come,' she said, going towards him. 'I was beginning to think—'

She stopped suddenly when she saw Godfrey's shaking hands and white face. She put her hand on his arm, but he did not seem to notice, and threw himself into a chair.

'Sit down—Nancy,' he said with difficulty. 'I came back as soon as I could, to prevent anyone telling you except me. It's terrible news for me, but I'm more worried about how *you* will feel about it.'

'It isn't father or Priscilla?' said Nancy, trying to control her trembling lips.

'No, it's nobody living,' said Godfrey. 'It's Dunstan, my brother, who left home sixteen years ago and never came back.

9　戈弗雷终于坦白了

红屋里，南茜正在耐心地等着戈弗雷回家来喝茶，突然一个用人闯进客厅，兴奋地喊："夫人，街上有好多人！大家全都在向采石场跑！可能出什么事儿了！"

"简，别那么激动，"南茜平静地说，"我想不会有什么重要的事。去拿茶来，戈弗雷先生快回来了。"可她心里对自己说，"千万别是戈弗雷有什么事儿！"

几分钟后，当戈弗雷进屋时，她长出了一口气。"亲爱的，谢天谢地，你回来了！"她走上前，"我开始在想……"

她猛地停了下来。她看到戈弗雷双手发抖，脸色惨白。南茜把手放在他臂上，可他好像没感觉。他跌坐在一把椅子上。

"坐下——南茜，"他艰难地说，"我尽可能快地赶回来，我真怕别人来告诉你。这对我是个可怕的消息，可我更担心你会怎么想。"

"是爸爸或普丽西拉吗?"南茜努力克制着嘴唇的抖动。

"不，不关活人的事儿，"戈弗雷说，"是我弟弟邓斯坦，他从16年前离家后一直没有

sitting-room *n*. 起居室，客厅。**accident** *n*. *event unexpected* 事故，突发事件。

We've found him ... found his body—all that's left of it—in the old quarry.'

Nancy felt calmer now. *That* was not terrible news.

'You know the men have been draining our fields near the quarry. Well, as a result, the quarry has suddenly gone dry, and we've found him lying at the bottom. We know it's him because he's wearing his watch and his rings.'

Godfrey paused. It was not easy to say what came next.

'Do you think he drowned himself?' asked Nancy, wondering why her husband was so shaken by the death of a brother he had never loved.

'No, he fell in,' replied Godfrey in a low voice. 'Dunstan was the man who robbed Silas Marner. The bags of gold were found with his body.'

'Oh Godfrey! I *am* sorry!' said Nancy. She understood how ashamed her husband must be. The Casses were so proud of their family name.

'I had to tell you. I couldn't keep it from you,' Godfrey continued, and then stopped, looking at the ground for two long minutes. Nancy knew that he had something more to say. Finally Godfrey lifted his eyes to her face, and said, 'Everybody's secrets are discovered sooner or later, Nancy. I've lived with a secret ever since I married you, but I'm going to confess it now. I don't want you to discover it from someone else, or hear about it when I'm dead. I was weak and hesitating when I was younger — I'm going to be firm with myself now.'

回来。我们找到他了……找到了他的尸体——所有剩下的部分——在采石场里。"

南茜平静多了，这并不是太可怕的消息。

"你知道我让人给我们采石场边上那几块地排水，结果采石场一下子被排干了，我们在坑底发现了他的尸体。我们从手表和戒指认出那是他。"

戈弗雷停了下来。要说出后面的事儿很不容易。

"他是自杀吗？"南茜不明白丈夫为什么会对那个他从来没喜欢过的弟弟的死而这样难过。

"不，他失足掉下去的，"戈弗雷低声说，"邓斯坦是那个偷西拉斯钱的人，从他身上找到了钱袋子。"

"噢，戈弗雷！我太难过了！"她知道丈夫一定感到非常耻辱。凯斯家族的荣誉是至高无尚的。

"我得告诉你，我不能向你隐瞒，"戈弗雷停下来，眼睛盯着地板看了两分钟。南茜知道他还有话要说。终于戈弗雷抬起了眼看着南茜的脸，说："每个人的秘密早晚都会被发现，南茜。我们结婚以后我一直隐藏着一个秘密，现在我要把它向你坦白。我不想让你从别人那里发现它，或是在我死了以后再听到它。年轻的时候我脆弱而且优柔寡断——现在我要坚强起来。"

bottom *n. lowest part of anything* 底部。**sooner or later** 早晚。

Nancy could not speak. She stared at her husband in horror. What secret could he possibly have from her?

'Nancy,' said Godfrey slowly, 'when I married you, I hid something from you — I was wrong not to tell you. That woman Silas Marner found dead in the snow — Eppie's mother — that poor woman — was my wife. Eppie is my child.'

He paused, looking worriedly at Nancy. But she sat quite still, although her face looked rather white.

'Perhaps you won't be able to love me any more,' he said, his voice trembling a little.

She was silent.

'I was wrong, I know I was wrong to marry Molly and then to keep it a secret. But I loved you, Nancy, I only ever wanted to marry you.'

Still Nancy was silent, looking down at her hands. And Godfrey almost expected her to get up and say she would leave him and go to live with her father and sister. She was so religious, and so firm in her ideas of right and wrong!

But at last she lifted her eyes to his and spoke. She did not sound angry, but only sad. 'Oh Godfrey, why didn't you tell me this long ago? I didn't know Eppie was yours and so I refused to adopt her. Of course I'd accept *your child* into our home! But — oh, Godfrey — how sad to think we've spent all these years with no children! Why didn't you confess the truth before we married? We could be so happy now, with a beautiful daughter, who would love me as her mother!' Tears

南茜害怕地看着丈夫，什么也说不出。他会隐瞒了什么呢？

“南茜，”戈弗雷慢慢地说，“娶你的时候，我隐瞒了些东西——我很不应该不告诉你。那个被西拉斯发现死在雪地上的可怜女人——埃比的妈妈——是我的妻子。埃比是我的孩子。”

他停下来，担心地看着南茜，可她仍然静静地坐着，只是脸更白了。

“你也许不会再爱我了。”他的声音有些发抖。

她沉默着。

“我错了，我知道我不该娶了莫丽而又不说出来。可我爱你，南茜，我只想娶你。”

南茜看着自己的手，仍然沉默着。戈弗雷想她一定会站起来说她要离开他去和父亲和姐姐生活在一起。她是那么的虔诚，那么的是非分明！

但最后南茜抬眼看着戈弗雷，声音悲伤，但并不愤怒：“戈弗雷，你怎么能那么长时间不告诉我呢？我不知道埃比是你的女儿，所以不同意领养她。我当然应当接纳你的孩子来我们的家。哦，戈弗雷——这么多年没有孩子是多不容易呀！为什么结婚前你不告诉我实情？那样我们多快活，会有一个漂亮的女儿，她会像爱她的妈妈那样爱我！”

religious *a. pious, believing in religion* 虔诚的。

were running down Nancy's face.

'But Nancy,' cried Godfrey, bitterly angry with himself, 'I couldn't tell you everything! I was in danger of losing you if I told you the truth!'

'I don't know about that, Godfrey. I certainly never wanted to marry anyone else. But it wasn't worth doing wrong just so that you could marry me. And our marriage hasn't been as happy for you as you thought it would be.' There was a sad smile on Nancy's face as she said the last words.

'Can you ever forgive me for what I've done, Nancy?'

'You have only hurt *me* a little, Godfrey, and you've been a good husband to me for fifteen years. But it's the other woman who you've hurt the most, and I don't see how you can put that right.'

'But we can take Eppie into our home now,' said Godfrey.

'It'll be different now that she's grown up,' said Nancy, shaking her head sadly. 'It'll be more difficult for her to get used to us. But it's our duty to take care of your child, and I'll ask God to make her love me.'

'Then we'll go to the weaver's cottage tonight,' said Godfrey, 'and talk to Marner and Eppie about it.'

泪水顺着南茜的脸颊流了下来。

“可是南茜,”戈弗雷对自己很气恼,“我不能告诉你这些!我怕说了实话我就会失去你!”

“我也不知道,戈弗雷,我从没想过要嫁给别人,可你不值得为娶我而做错事,而且我们的婚姻也不像你想的那么幸福。”说到最后南茜苦笑了一下。

“你能宽恕我所做的吗,南茜?”

“你对我的伤害并不严重,况且你已经做了 15 年的好丈夫。可你对另一个女人的伤害最重,我不知道你能怎么去弥补。”

“我们可以去把埃比接到家里来。”戈弗雷说。

“这并不那么容易,因为她已经长大了,”南茜悲哀地摇着头,“接受我们对她更难。可我们有义务去照料你的孩子,我会求上帝让她爱我。”

“那我们今晚就去织布匠的家,”戈弗雷说,“去对西拉斯和埃比说。”

forgive *v. to say or show that you are not angry with sb.* 饶恕。

10

Eppie has to decide

That evening Silas was resting in his chair near the fire, after the excitement of the day. Eppie was sitting close to him, holding both his hands, and on the table was Silas's lost gold. He had put the coins in piles, as he used to.

'You see, that's all I ever did in the long evenings before you came to me,' he was telling Eppie, 'just count my gold. I was only half alive in those days. What a good thing the money was taken away from me! I was killing myself with working all day, and counting money half the night. It wasn't a healthy life. And when you came, with your yellow curls, I thought *you* were the gold. And then, when I began to love you, I didn't want my gold any more.' He stopped talking for a moment and looked at the money. 'The gold doesn't mean anything to me now. But perhaps, if I ever lost you, Eppie, if you ever went away from me, I'd need my gold again. I'd feel lonely then, and I'd think God had forgotten me, and perhaps I'd go back to my bad old habits.'

There were tears in Eppie's beautiful eyes, but she did not have time to answer Silas, as just then there was a knock on the door. When she opened it, Mr and Mrs Godfrey Cass came in.

'Good evening, my dear,' said Nancy, taking Eppie's hand gently. 'We're sorry to come so late.'

10 埃比需要做出选择

晚上，一天的忙碌过后，西拉斯坐在炉火旁的椅子上休息，埃比拉着他的手坐在他旁边，西拉斯丢的金子放在桌子上。他像从前一样把金币码成一摞一摞的。

“你看，你来之前，我每天晚上就是这样做的，”他给埃比讲，“只是数我的金子。那时我只有半条生命。金子被偷走对我来说真是件好事！那时我在用整天工作，整晚上数钱的方法自杀。那是不健康的生活。你来的时候，因为你的金黄的头发，我把你当成了金子。后来，当我开始爱你，我就不再想什么金子了。”他停了一会儿，看着金子，“现在金子对我毫无意义了，可是一旦失去你，埃比，或是你离我而去，我会重新需要金子。那时我会感到孤独，我会觉得自己被上帝抛弃了，可能我会回到以前的样子。”

埃比美丽的眼睛里充满了泪水，可她还没来得及回答西拉斯就响起了敲门声。她打开门，戈弗雷·凯斯先生和太太进到屋里来。

“晚上好，亲爱的，”南茜轻轻拉着埃比的手，“抱歉我们这么晚来。”

excitement *n*. 忙乱，忙碌。

'Well, Marner,' said Godfrey, as he and Nancy sat down, 'I'm glad you've got your money back, and I'm very sorry it was one of my family who stole it from you. Whatever I can do for you, I will, to repay what I owe you — and I owe you a lot, Marner.'

Silas was always uncomfortable with important people like the young Squire. 'You don't owe me anything, sir. You've already been very kind to me. And that money on the table is more than most working people can save in their whole life. Eppie and I don't need very much.'

Godfrey was impatient to explain why they had come. 'Yes, you've done well these last sixteen years, Marner, taking care of Eppie here. She looks pretty and healthy, but not very strong. Don't you think she should be a lady, not a working woman? Now Mrs Cass and I, you know, have no children, and we'd like to adopt a daughter to live with us in our beautiful home and enjoy all the good things we're used to. In fact, we'd like to have Eppie. I'm sure you'd be glad to see her become a lady, and of course we'd make sure *you* have everything you need. And Eppie will come to see you very often, I expect.'

Godfrey did not find it easy to say what he felt, and as a result his words were not chosen sensitively. Silas was hurt, and afraid. His whole body trembled as he said quietly to Eppie after a moment, 'I won't stand in your way, my child. Thank Mr and Mrs Cass. It's very kind of them.'

"你好,马南,"戈弗雷一边说,一边和南茜坐下来,"恭喜你找回你的钱。我很惭愧是我们家里的人偷了你的钱。我会尽一切力量去补偿你,马南,我欠你太多了。"

西拉斯一向不擅于和像年轻的乡绅这样重要的人物相处。"你不欠我什么,先生,你一直对我很好,桌上的钱已经比好多人一辈子攒的钱都多了,我和埃比并不需要很多东西。"

戈弗雷急着向西拉斯解释今天的来意。"是的,马南,你这16年来对埃比照顾得非常好,她又漂亮又健康,只是不太强壮。你难道不觉得她应该成为一个淑女而不是个整天干活的人吗?你知道凯斯太太和我没有孩子,我们想收养个女儿,让她和我们生活在一起,住漂亮的房子,享受所有的好东西。实际上我们想收养埃比,我想你会乐意看到埃比成为一位淑女,而且我保证给你你想要的一切,而且我想埃比也会经常回来看你的。"

戈弗雷一时不知用什么词语才能表达自己的感受,结果他用词很不慎重。西拉斯既气愤又害怕,过了一会儿,他全身颤抖着对埃比轻声说:"我不会挡你的路,我的孩子。谢谢凯斯先生和太太,他们的心地很好。"

sensitive *a. easily hurt* 敏感的。

Eppie stepped forward. She was blushing, but held her head high. 'Thank you, sir and madam. But I can't leave my father. And I don't want to be a lady, thank you.' She went back to Silas's chair, and put an arm round his neck, brushing the tears from her eyes.

Godfrey was extremely annoyed. He wanted to do what he thought was his duty. And adopting Eppie would make him feel much less guilty about his past. 'But, Eppie, you *must* agree,' he cried. '*You are my daughter*! Marner, Eppie's my own child. Her mother was my wife.'

Eppie's face went white. Silas, who had been relieved by hearing Eppie's answer to Godfrey, now felt angry. 'Then, sir,' he answered bitterly, 'why didn't you confess this sixteen years ago, before I began to love her? Why do you come to take her away now, when it's like taking the heart out of my body? God gave her to me because you turned your back on her! And He considers her mine!'

'I know I was wrong, and I'm sorry,' said Godfrey. 'But be sensible, Marner! She'll be very near you and will often come to see you. She'll feel just the same towards you.'

'Just the same?' said Silas more bitterly than ever. 'How *can* she feel the same? We're used to spending all our time together! We need each other!'

Godfrey thought the weaver was being very selfish. 'I think, Marner,' he said firmly, 'that you should consider what's best for Eppie. You shouldn't stand in her way, when

埃比走上前。她的脸很红,可还是努力高昂着头。"谢谢你们,先生、太太,可我不能离开我的爸爸,而且我也不想做什么淑女。谢谢你们。"她说完走回到西拉斯的椅子旁,一只胳膊搂着西拉斯的脖子,拂去眼里的泪水。

戈弗雷被彻底搞烦了,他想履行他心目中自己的责任,而且收养埃比会减轻一些他对过去的负罪感。"可你必须同意,埃比,"他嚷了起来,"你是我的女儿!马南,她是我的孩子,她妈妈是我的妻子。"

埃比的脸变得惨白,刚刚为埃比的回答感到欣慰的西拉斯此时愤怒了。"那么先生,"他痛苦地说,"那你为什么不在16年前,我还没有开始爱她的时候承认?为什么你现在来把她带走,像挖走我的心一样?上帝把她给了我,因为你不要她!上帝认为她是我的!"

"我知道我错了,我很抱歉,"戈弗雷说,"可你理智点儿,马南,她会离你很近而且会常来看你,她对你的感情也会和以前一样。"

"一样?"西拉斯更痛苦了,"怎么会和以前一样?我们所有的时间都在一起,习惯了!我们不能分开!"

戈弗雷认为织布匠太自私了。"我认为,马南,"他坚决地说,"你得想想怎么样对埃比最好。你不应该妨碍她去过更好的生活。

annoy *v. make rather angry* 使烦恼,使生气。**selfish** *a. thinking chielfly of one's personal interest* 自私的。

she could have a better life. I'm sorry, but I think it's my duty to take care of my own daughter.'

Silas was silent for a moment. He was worried that perhaps Godfrey was right, and that it was selfish of him to keep Eppie. At last he made himself bring out the difficult words. 'All right. I'll say no more. Speak to the child. I won't prevent her from going.'

Godfrey and Nancy were relieved to hear this, and thought that Eppie would now agree. 'Eppie, my dear,' said Godfrey, 'althought I haven't been a good father to you so far, I want to do my best for you now. And my wife will be the best of mothers to you.'

'I've always wanted a daughter, my dear,' added Nancy in her gentle voice.

But Eppie did not come forward this time. She stood by Silas's side, holding his hand in hers, and spoke almost coldly. 'Thank you, sir and madam, for your kind offer. But I wouldn't be happy if I left father. He'd have nobody if I weren't here. Nobody shall ever come between him and me!'

'But you must make sure, Eppie,' said Silas worriedly, 'that you won't be sorry, if you decide to stay with poor people. You could have a much better life at the Red House.'

'I'll never be sorry, father,' said Eppie firmly. 'I don't want to be rich, if I can't live with the people I know and love.'

Nancy thought she could help to persuade Eppie. 'What you

我很抱歉,可我想照顾我自己的女儿是我的责任。"

西拉斯沉默了一会儿,他也担心或许戈弗雷是对的,自己留下埃比是不是太自私了。终于他艰难地说:"好吧,我不再说了,你对孩子说吧。她要走,我不会拦着。"

听到这些,戈弗雷和南茜舒了一口气,他们想这回埃比该同意了。"亲爱的埃比,"戈弗雷说,"我虽然以前没有做个好父亲,可我今后会尽所有努力对你好,我的妻子也会成为你最好的母亲 。"

"我一直想要一个女儿,亲爱的。"南茜轻声说。

这回埃比没有走上前。她站在西拉斯的旁边,拉着他的手,冷冷地说:"谢谢你们的好意,先生太太,可我离开爸爸就不会再感到幸福。我不在这儿,他就谁也没有了。没有人能把我们分开。"

"但你必须肯定,埃比,"西拉斯担心地说,"你留下和穷人在一起不会后悔。到红屋你会过得好得多。"

"我永远也不后悔,爸爸,"埃比坚决地说,"如果不能和我了解的、我爱的人在一起,我不会渴望富有。"

南茜想自己应当帮着劝劝埃比。"你说

duty *n*. 责任。

say is natural, my dear child,' she said kindly. 'But there's a duty you owe to your lawful father. If he opens his home to you, you shouldn't turn your back on him.'

'But I can't think of any home except this one!' cried Eppie, tears running down her face. 'I've only ever known one father! And I've promised to marry a working man, who'll live with us, and help me take care of father!'

Godfrey looked at Nancy. 'Let's go,' he said to her bitterly, in a low voice.

'We won't talk of this any more,' said Nancy, getting up. 'We just want the best for you, Eppie my dear, and you too, Marner. Good night.'

Nancy and Godfrey left the cottage and walked home in the moonlight. When they reached home, Godfrey dropped into a chair. Nancy stood near him, waiting for him to speak. After a few moments he looked up at her, and took her hand.

'That's ended!' he said sadly.

She kissed him and then said, 'Yes, I'm afraid we can't hope to adopt her, if she doesn't want to come to us.'

'No,' said Godfrey, 'it's too late now. I made mistakes in the past, and I can't put them right. I wanted to be childless once, Nancy, and now I'll always be childless.'

He thought for a moment, and then spoke in a softer voice. 'But I got *you*, Nancy, and yet I've been wanting something different all the time. Perhaps from now on I'll be able to accept our life better, and we'll be happier.'

的很自然,我的孩子。"她慈爱地说,"可你对你的生父也有义务。他把家门为你打开,你不该不理睬他。"

"可我除这儿之外没有别的家。"埃比泪流满面,"我只知道一个爸爸,而且我已经决定要嫁给一个普通人,他会和我们生活在一起,和我一起照料爸爸。"

戈弗雷看着南茜。"我们走吧!"他低声说,声音很苦涩。

"我们不会再提这件事,"南茜站起身,"我们只希望你们好,亲爱的埃比,还有你,马南。晚安!"

南茜和戈弗雷离开小屋,踏着月色回到家。一进家门,戈弗雷就跌坐在椅子里,南茜站在他旁边,等着他开口,过了一会儿,他抬起头,拉着她的手。

"全完了!"他伤心地说。

她吻了吻他,然后说:"是的,我想她不想和我们走,我们就不可能收养她了。"

"现在太晚了,"戈弗雷说,"我过去做了错事,现在已经不可能弥补了,我曾希望没有孩子,南茜,但现在,我将永远没有孩子了。"

想了一会儿,戈弗雷用更轻柔的声音说:"可我得到了你,南茜,但我总想要更新鲜的东西。也许从现在起,我更能够接受我们的生活,我们会更快活。"

natural *a*. *normal* 自然的,正常的。**lawful** *a*. *recognized by law*, *legal* 合法的,法定的。**drop into** *fell into* 跌入,落入。

The following spring, there was a wedding in Raveloe. The sun shone warmly as Eppie walked through the village towards the church, with Silas, Aaron and Dolly. Eppie was wearing the beautiful white wedding dress she had always dreamed of, which Nancy Cass had bought for her. She was walking arm in arm with her father, Silas.

'I promise nothing will change when I'm married, father,' she whispered to him as they entered the church. 'You know I'll never leave you.'

There was quite a crowd of villagers outside the church to see the wedding. Just then Miss Priscilla Lammeter and her father drove into the village.

'Look, father!' cried Priscilla. 'How lucky! We're in time to see the weaver's daughter getting married! Doesn't she look lovely? I'm sorry Nancy couldn't find a pretty little orphan girl like that to take care of.'

'Yes, my dear,' agreed Mr Lammeter. 'Now that we're all getting older, it would be good to have a young one in the family. Unfortunately, it's too late now.'

They went into the Red House, where Nancy was waiting for them. They had come to spend the day with her, because Godfrey was away on business and she would perhaps be lonely without him. The Casses were not going to Eppie's wedding.

When the little wedding group came out of the church, the villagers and Silas's family all went to the Rainbow. There a wonderful wedding lunch was waiting for them, which had

第二年春天，一个婚礼在瑞福洛举行。与西拉斯、阿荣和多莉一起，埃比在暖融融的阳光里穿过村子走向教堂。埃比穿着南茜·凯斯为她买来的、她一直梦想能穿的美丽洁白的婚纱，她的爸爸西拉斯挽着她的胳膊。

“我保证结婚后什么都不会变，爸爸，”进教堂时她对西拉斯耳语，“我永远不会离开你。”

教堂外面很多人来参加婚礼，这时拉默特先生和普丽西拉正乘车走进村子。

“看，父亲！”普丽西拉叫着，“多幸运！我们正赶上织布匠女儿的婚礼！她真可爱！可惜南茜没有收养到一个这样可爱的小孤女。”

“是的，亲爱的。”拉默特应和道，“我们都老了，家里是应该有个小家伙。可惜现在太晚了。”

到红屋时，南茜正在等他们。他们来就是为了陪她。因为戈弗雷外出办事了，南茜也许会很寂寞。凯斯家的人没有参加埃比的婚礼。

仪式进行完，西拉斯一家人和村民们都从教堂出来走进了小酒馆。戈弗雷·凯斯

wedding *n. a ceremony through which a man and a woman become husband and wife* 婚礼。**a crowd of** *a group of (people)* 一群（人）。

been ordered and paid for by Godfrey Cass.

'It's very generous of the young Squire to pay for all this,' said the landlord as he refilled the beer glasses.

'Well, what would you expect?' replied old Mr Macey sharply. 'Remember, it was his own brother who stole the weaver's gold! And Mr Godfrey has always helped Master Marner, with furniture and clothes and so on, since young Eppie came to the cottage. Well, it's only right to help a man like Master Marner. And I'd like you all to remember — I was the first to tell you I thought Master Marner was harmless — and I was right! Now let's drink to the health of the happy young couple!' And the villagers lifted their glasses and cried, 'To Eppie and Aaron!'

When the meal was over and the guests had begun to return to their homes, Silas, Eppie and her new husband walked slowly back to their cottage by the quarry. It had been enlarged by Godfrey Cass's workmen, and was looking lovely in the late afternoon sunshine.

'Oh father,' said Eppie. 'What a pretty home ours is! I think nobody could be happier than we are!'

在这里为他们订下了一桌丰盛的酒席。

“乡绅真大方，花钱办这酒席。”酒馆主人边添啤酒边说。

“你以为呢?”麦西先生尖刻地说，“记住，是他弟弟偷了人家织布匠的金子！而且自从埃比到了小屋，戈弗雷先生经常帮助马南师傅，给他衣服、家具什么的。帮助一个像马南师傅这样的人是对的。我想你们都应当记得是我最先说马南师傅不是坏人的——我是对的！现在让我们为新人的健康干杯!”村民们都举起杯喊：“为埃比和阿荣干杯!”

当酒席结束，客人们已开始回家的时候，西拉斯与埃比和她的新婚丈夫一起慢慢走回他们在采石场边上的小屋，小屋已经被戈弗雷·凯斯的工人们扩大了，在下午的阳光下显得格外可爱。

“哦，爸爸，”埃比说，“我们的家多么可爱呀！我想我们是世界上最幸福的人!”

generous *a. noble-minded, willing to give* 慷慨的，大方的。**refill** *v. fill again* 重新倒满，重新装满。**enlarge** *v. make larger* 扩大。

Exercises

A Checking your understanding

Chapters 1—2 *Write answers to these questions.*

1 Why were the Raveloe villagers afraid of Silas Marner?

2 Where had Silas come from?

3 Why did Silas have to leave the chapel and his friends there?

4 Who do you think stole the money which Silas was accused of taking?

5 What was Godfrey's secret?

6 Why did Dunstan ride Godfrey's horse to the hunt?

7 Why was Silas's door unlocked when Dunstan visited his cottage?

Chapters 3—4 *Are these sentences true (T) or false (F)?*

1 Silas kept his gold locked in a cupboard.

2 He suspected Jem Rodney the poacher of stealing his gold.

3 The villagers also suspected the poacher.

4 When Dunstan did not come home after the hunt, his family was very worried.

5 Godfrey did not tell the Squire the whole truth.

6 The Squire did not want Godfrey to marry Nancy Lammeter.

Chapters 5—7 *How much can you remember? Check your answers.*

1 Which villagers came to visit Silas and cheer him up?

2 What was the best party of the year in Raveloe?

3 Who did Godfrey ask for the first dance?

4 What did Silas feel when he reached out his hand to his 'gold'?

5 How many people knew the name of the dead woman in the snow?

6 What name did Silas give the child, and why?

Chapters 8—10 *Find answers to these questions in the text.*

1 What was the great sadness of Nancy's married life?

2 What did Eppie tell Silas when they were sitting outside the cottage?

3 What was found in the quarry?

4 Why did Godfrey finally confess his secret to Nancy?

5 Why didn't Eppie want the Casses to adopt her?

B Working with language

1 *Complete these sentences with information from the story.*

1 Every night Silas counted his gold coins because...

2 The Squire was very angry when...

3 Dolly wanted Silas to go to church on Christmas Day but...

4 Godfrey could not marry Nancy unless...

5 Silas's life changed completely after...

2 *Put this summary into the right order and then make four sentences. Check your answers in Chapter 2.*

1 and sold him to a neighbour for a good price

2 as Dunstan was walking home after the accident

3 Dunstan rode Godfrey's horse Wildfire to the hunt
4 so he decided to search for Silas's gold
5 then he joined the other riders in the fields
6 he went in and saw that Silas was not at home
7 he saw the light from Silas's cottage through the mist
8 but poor Wildfire fell at a gate and broke his back

C Activities

1 You are a newspaper reporter. Write a report to describe how Dunstan Cass's body was found in the quarry, with the two bags of gold.

2 Imagine that Silas Marner decides to return to the town where he used to live. He visits the chapel minister, to discover if Mr Paston still thinks he was guilty of stealing the money thirty years ago. Write the conversation they have.

3 '*I don't want to be rich, if I can't live with the people I know and love.*' Do you agree with Eppie? Or do you think she would have a better life with the Casses at the Red House? Write a paragraph, saying what you would do in her situation.

书虫·牛津英汉对照读物(50种)

《哈克贝利·费恩历险记》
《爱丽丝漫游奇境记》
《鲁宾孙漂流记》
《弗兰肯斯坦》
《野性的呼唤》
《大卫·科波菲尔》
《威廉·莎士比亚》
《远大前程》
《巴斯克维尔猎犬》
《呼啸山庄》
《五个孩子和沙精》
《爱丽丝镜中世界奇遇记》
《圣诞欢歌》
《诱拐》
《黑骏马》
《歌剧院的幽灵》
《化学秘密》
《格林·盖布尔斯来的安妮》
《猴爪》
《一个国王的爱情故事》
《多里安·格雷的画像》
《神秘幻想故事集》
《公正》
《三怪客泛舟记》
《织工马南》
《傲慢与偏见》
《苏格兰玛丽女王》
《双城记》
《爱情与金钱》
《格列佛游记》
《雾都孤儿》
《小妇人》
《远离尘嚣》
《简·爱》
《苔丝》
《秘密花园》
《风语河岸柳》
《曾达的囚徒》
《金银岛》
《象人》
《星际动物园》
《在月亮下面》
《潘德尔的巫师》
《世界上最冷的地方》
《亡灵岛》
《勃朗特一家的故事》
《牙齿和爪子》
《不平静的坟墓》
《三十九级台阶》
《化身博士》